"You're dead, Leatherhand!"

one of them shouted gleefully and died instead, as Vent shot him in the face, the heavy slug driving him back and over the rump of his horse. Arbuckle, still in the fight, killed another and Vent triggered twice, sending twin streaks of fire into the bodies of the two remaining gunmen, dropping one directly into the fire. The coffee pot upended and smoke poured from the wet wood and then Sharp whirled into the clearing leading Vent's Appaloosa and shouted, "Vent, Borden's dead and The Preacher's on the run. Let's hit it!"

Running to Arbuckle, Vent grasped the gunman under the arms, then cursed wildly when his left arm wouldn't cooperate. Arbuckle looked up at Vent and said distinctly, "Hell of a fight we got goin here, ain't it?" and blood poured from his mouth and he coughed once and was suddenly a dead weight leaning against Vent.

LEATHERHAND

#3: LOTTERY OF DEATH

MIKE WALES

PINNACLE BOOKS   **NEW YORK**

This is a work of fiction. All the characters and events portrayed in
this book are fictional, and any resemblance to real people or
incidents is purely coincidental.

LEATHERHAND #3: LOTTERY OF DEATH

Copyright © 1984 by Mike Wales

An original Pinnacle Books edition, published for the first time
anywhere.

First printing / March 1984

ISBN: 0-523-42157-5

Can. ISBN: 0-523-43147-3

Cover art by Bruce Minney

Printed in the United States of America

PINNACLE BOOKS, INC.
1430 Broadway
New York, New York 10018

9 8 7 6 5 4 3 2

LOTTERY OF DEATH

Chapter One

The game had started when the train pulled away from Dodge City belching a black column of soot-filled smoke and lined out down the narrow gage track on its way to Denver. The five men sitting around the table represented enough money to almost buy the mile high city the train was just now approaching.

Stiles Burlingame-Leach owned five of the biggest silver mines in Colorado, second only to the holdings of the fabulous Silver King of Leadville, Horace Tabor. Burlingame-Leach had been sent to the United States by his highly placed English family after he repeatedly disgraced them by showing an uncommon bent for women, wine and song, in that order.

For five years he trudged through the hills of Colorado in search of the lode that always seemed to be just up the next gulch. Then, when he was almost at the end of both his financial rope, having mortgaged his remittance from England for a year ahead, and his physical rope, he stum-

1

bled onto one of the richest silver mines in Colorado. What followed was another story of rags to riches.

Now Burlingame-Leach stared morosely at his cards, knitted his brow, and seeing he had drawn a deuce and tray in an attempt to fill a three-card straight, grunted with disgust and tossed in his hand. Staring across the table at Johnny ''Tombstone'' Morgan from a pair of gun-metal eyes shrouded by arching eyebrows as red as cinnabar, he twisted his mouth around the blunt end of his cigar and waited for Morgan to bet.

Morgan was another self-made man. He had gotten his start in lumber, and through shrewd business sense and a knack for taking the right chance had amassed a fortune by providing the mines with timbers cut from the slopes of the Colorado Rockies and hauled aboard long, hardwood-bedded wagons drawn by teams of mules. When the railroads started driving west, Morgan capitalized on his already thriving business by landing a dozen contracts to provide cross ties. Then he diversified, buying hotels and gambling joints from Leadville to Denver. Everything he touched seemed to turn into money and most of it stuck to his fingers.

He was nicknamed Tombstone after he appeared in that town in Arizona out of nowhere, sat in a poker game with a five-dollar gold piece, earned making a tombstone for a recent widow, and walked out with four thousand dollars in cash and the deed to a bankrupt sawmill near Steamboat Springs. Using the cash to put the mill back on its financial legs, Morgan parlayed it into a dozen more mills. On this day, as he peeked at his cards, noting the three aces sitting all in a row, he was worth well over five million dollars. Now he bet a thousand dollars.

Amos Dewberry, whose turn it was to call, did not

flinch. He would not have flinched if the bet had been twenty times a thousand. Dewberry owned over 70,000 acres of Colorado ranch land and 35,000 head of prime beef. His holdings reached from Colorado Springs to Wild Horse and it was said of him that he could furnish mounts for the entire Fifth Cavalry and never miss them from his huge remudas.

Looking at Morgan he smiled dryly, burped softly and said, "Call," then covered the bet, glancing once at his three sevens.

The player to his left was a narrow-shouldered white-haired man with cold, penetrating eyes that missed nothing at that table. He was the only man in the room who wore a gun and it hung almost awkwardly from his lank frame. Rising, he removed his long-tailed coat, sat back down, carefully counted out two thousand dollars and tossed it wordlessly into the pot.

Deak Hammer owned the Bank of Denver, a share in two railroads, including the one they were riding on, and a gold mine in Nevada that some said was as rich as the Lost Dutchman in Arizona was reputed to be.

Hammer was known as a hard man with a dollar, however, his one failing was an almost obsessive love of gambling. Unlike many men addicted to the pasteboards or horses, Hammer seldom lost. He regarded each dollar anted into a pot as an investment, just as he regarded each dollar invested by his bank as money that would double itself and return to his coffers. Most of the time his poker investments did just that.

The short, fat man next to him frowned and rolled his cigar from his right cheek to his left, turned and fired into a spitoon without removing the weed, then glanced at his cards, carefully fanning them so the neat line of spades sat edge to edge in his hand and assured him his bet would bring home the pot.

Jake Sunderman owned a slaughterhouse in Denver, a second one in Chicago and 50,000 acres of ranch land in Montana. He kept track of his far-flung operations by moving from state to state on trains; when the track ran out, he took to a wagon, buggy or horseback. He never carried a gun, but then he didn't have to. Leaning against the wall near the door was his gun hand, a lean, tough man from Waco, Texas, who had buried half a dozen men during his short twenty-seven year life span. Now he worked for Sunderman and men walked shy of him once they heard the name Tonto McCord.

The bets in, Sunderman carefully spread his hand on the felt and said quietly, "Read 'em and weep, boys."

Hammer stared at Sunderman's king-high straight and cursed. The others merely grunted and tossed in their cards, watching the fat man rake in his winnings.

It was Morgan's deal, and as he shuffled the cards he asked casually, "You fellers hear about the shoot-out in Dodge last week?"

"Hell, they's a shoot-out in that town three times a week," Dewberry observed, raking in his cards as they snicked across the table and came to a sliding stop in front of him.

"This time it wasn't just a bunch of drunk cowpokes," Morgan grunted, dealing another round. "They was an argument in The Lady Gay between Ernie Cadwell and a hunchbacked feller. The hunchback drew and killed Cadwell before Ernie even got his gun out. They say it was the fastest draw anyone in that town had ever seen."

Sunderman turned and asked McCord, "Tonto, you ever hear anything about a hunchback lead tosser?"

McCord, his gravelly voice a metallic saw over the rattle of the train wheels, said, "That'd be Coup Arbuckle. A damn fast man."

"They say he went and spit in Cadwell's face after he plugged him," Morgan said, and dealt around the fifth card.

"He's a damn mean man, too," McCord grated.

Glancing at him curiously, Dewberry asked, "Can you beat him, Tonto?"

"Nope," the gravelly voiced guard answered. "Fact is, I don't know anyone who could shy that feller in a standup fight, and that includes Bill Longley or John Hardin."

"What about Owney Sharp?" Burlingame-Leach wanted to know.

"Good, but I doubt he can take the hunchback," McCord countered.

"I'd bet my money on Slab Borden," Hammer said.

Morgan grinned but the facial change did not quite reach his eyes. "My money would be on Angel Augustino," he said, and picked up his cards, glanced at them and tossed a fifty-dollar gold piece in the pot.

"Me, I'd go along with Tonto," Sunderman said. "If it came to a bet, I'd take the hunchback."

Dewberry looked at his cards, grunted in disgust as he threw them away, then said, "My choice would be Owney Sharp. I saw him come up against a couple of fellers in a game over to Leadville two years ago. Nailed them both before either man could get his gun into play."

"Ain't he a friend of that Missourian, Leatherhand?" Hammer asked, betting a hundred dollars that he would turn his one-card draw into a straight.

"Yep," Tonto McCord said. "He sided Leatherhand down in the Verde Valley against Gray Taper."

"I remember that fight," Morgan said around his cigar. "Old man Taper wound up hanging from his own noose."

Leach fingered his cards, then said absently, "I guess I'd have to bet on Leatherhand. Never saw him in a fight, but I've heard plenty."

Hammer filled out his straight and won the pot. Raking in the chips, he said mildly, "Seems when you got a difference of opinion, it makes for a bet. How about this; we each back our chosen man with ten thousand dollars. Whoever's left wins the bet, which means his backer takes all."

Morgan stared at him. "How the hell you gonna get five men to shoot each other?"

Dewberry shifted his 210 pounds in his chair and snuffing loudly, proclaimed, "Hell, I'd back Owney Sharp against any two of those boys."

Hammer, who had been thinking about it carefully, now looked up and said, "You fellers remember the town of Dead End?"

Sunderman nodded as he dealt the cards in another round. "Ain't that that old mining town that turned ghost about five years ago when pay dirt played out?"

"That's it," Hammer said. "I propose we offer each one of these fellers five thousand dollars to show up at Dead End and whoever rides out of there gets all the money."

Each man sat staring at his cards, thinking it over. None of them was morally against the idea of setting five gunmen against each other. Their one concern was, had they chosen their champion well?

Now Hammer spoke again. "Each of us must also be responsible for getting his choice to go to Dead End."

"Hell, that shouldn't be a problem," Morgan observed.

"That's more money than any of those boys has earned in his lifetime."

Sunderman shook his head doubtfully. "We might talk the hunchback and Borden into going, but I'm not that sure about Owney Sharp or this feller Leatherhand."

"What's Leatherhand's real name?" Dewberry asked.

Leach looked up from his cards and, speaking in his precise English fashion, said, "It's Vent Torrey. They call him Leatherhand because of a contraption he wears on his gun hand. I heard some Indian invented it for him after he got shot through the hand and couldn't use it anymore."

"I heard that story too," Morgan said, and bet five hundred dollars. "He got shot all to hell over near Dodge in a fight with the Hawks family. The Torreys and the Hawkses was from Missouri and they been feuding for more years than anybody down there can recall. They say Torrey hunted down the Hawkses after he mended and killed them all."

"Not all of them," Leach said. "I heard he left old man Hawks alive but crippled."

Morgan glanced over his cards at Leach and asked, "How come you want him?"

Leach smiled. "He's killed some of the best gunmen in the West. They say he can't be beaten and I believe it enough to risk my money on him."

"What if he refuses to take part in our little game?" Sunderman wantd to know.

"Why, I suppose I'll just have to convince him, now won't I?" Leach said and tossed a thousand dollars in the pot.

Hammer grinned as he called the bet. "I won't have any problem getting Borden to show up. That feller hates everybody. He'll go just so he can kill the rest of them."

"I heard he and the hunchback got a long-standing grudge against each other," Morgan said.

"Should make the game all that more interesting," Leach noted.

"They'll make good targets for Augstino," Morgan grinned. "Hell, that Mex has put more than twenty men in the graveyard."

"He's a bad one, all right," Dewberry agreed, and carefully spread his hand on the felt. When the other players threw away their losing cards, he raked in the pot with satisfaction.

"Then we've got us a bet?" Sunderman asked.

"We got a bet," Morgan agreed as he tilted his stove-pipe hat back on his head and ran a square-knuckled hand over his whiskery face.

"Let's set a limit on getting our men to Dead End," Leach suggested.

"Good idea," Hammer agreed. "Why not make it one month from today?"

The men glanced at a calendar on the wall, noted it was June 3, 1880, and nodded as one man. Morgan rose and, walking to the calendar, flipped the page to July and, taking a stub of a pencil from the pocket of his baggy pants, carefully drew a circle around the three, then tore out the page and handed it to McCord.

"Hang on to this, Tonto," he said, and McCord carefully folded the sheet and put it in his vest pocket.

Then the train began slowing down and Morgan braced himself against the wall as the jerky slowdown threatened to spill him off his feet.

"Reckon we're in Denver," Morgan said.

*   *   *

The town of Dead End lay high in the Medicine Bow Mountains west of Fort Collins. It clung precariously to the slopes of a narrow canyon that had once produced enough gold to warrant daily visits by the Overland Stage Company, the construction of a bank, now a barely recognizable ruin, and a dozen saloons. There was no church. Dead End had not been that kind of town. Where most of the mining towns of the west in the late 1800s were built with a distinct dividing line separating the bad element from the good citizen, Dead End was different. According to the old-timers, it was all bad.

There were two level spots in the town. One was the main street, which ran north and south, bisected by a narrow-gage railroad line, and the other was the cemetery, located on a small shelf just south of town and a hundred feet above the town proper. Its tombstones and broken wooden crosses were the first thing a visitor saw upon riding into Dead End.

Many of the buildings still remained standing and some, such as the hotel, were habitable. The old jail, constructed from heavy logs chinked with clay, stood like a solid symbol of justice at the head of Main Street, placed there by the businessmen of the town in hopes of impressing the tougher element. The latter had ignored it.

Shootings occurred almost daily and the lone doctor was kept busy sewing up knife slashes and digging bullets from the bodies of the survivors. In most cases, gunfights took place at brutally close range, and as often as not both participants wound up in adjoining graves, or if the gravedigger happened to be drunk that day, in the same hole. Not only did it save space and labor but such a grave only required one marker.

There were the remnants of a Chinese laundry sitting ear

to ear with an assay office where rock samples and chunks of ore lay scattered around the steps and on the packed earth floor. To the east of the town, and separated from it by a hundred yards of rocky slope, stood a huge, two-story house, all gables and dormer windows. The ground floor was surrounded by a wide verandah-type porch. A large set of double doors led into the interior where the elite of the town used to dance away the hours celebrating their luck in having hit pay dirt.

The house had belonged to Silas Carpenter, long since gone to his reward. It was he who had discovered the first color in Bobcat Creek, a rambunctious stream that slashed its way down canyon, running parallel to the rear of the business establishments and furnishing a convenient garbage-disposal system. There were bridges spanning the creek extending from behind many of the buildings, each leading to a corral and crude horse shelter on the higher side of the creek.

Carpenter, a solitary man who wandered the Colorado Rockies for ten years searching for that elusive strike, turned into just the opposite kind of man when he struck it rich. He staked his claim, then immediately announced its discovery in Fort Collins, a declaration that almost emptied the fort and was responsible for at least forty desertions from the fort's troop compliment.

The result was a booming gold town that seemed to spring up in that lonely canyon as if by magic. And Silas Carpenter gloried in it. It was as if he had at last found a way to guarantee companionship, something he never had in all the years he hunted gold.

Two months after he built the big house on the hill, he went to Denver and returned two weeks later with a sixteen-year-old bride. Silas was fifty-one.

Now his dreams and the dreams of all those who followed his boot tracks up Bobcat Creek were over. Some had remained to help fill the cemetery. Others had moved on to bigger and better strikes.

A year before the pay dirt played out, the town's more responsible citizens, tired of ducking random shots fired by drunken miners, gunfighting gamblers and bullwhackers, hired themselves a marshal. Within two weeks he increased the population of the cemetery by seven men, and after that, things quieted down.

Now the marshal's office faced the street in bleak abandon, its twin windows framing a door hanging by leather-strap hinges, its interior dusty and occupied only by spiders whose webs hung over everything. A battered desk squatted in the center of the room and a wooden file cabinet pushed against a back wall. A gun rack, its rifle slots empty, hung from the west wall near a poster board still cluttered with old wanted dodgers, among them one that offered twenty thousand dollars for the capture of the James boys, dead or alive.

The man who had occupied this office during the camp's heyday sat a big black horse high on the west rim of the canyon above the town and gazed down at the miniature buildings. He let his eyes wander across to the opposite canyon wall and finally around to stop as he carefully examined the end of the canyon where the creek suddenly belched from a hole at the base of a sheer cliff.

If it hadn't been for the twin .45s the man wore in a pair of half-breed holsters, he could have passed for a circuit-riding preacher of the day. His coat was long, black and had seen better days. The eyes that examined the empty town were hard, bleak and filled with a great knowledge of death, hate and man's foolishness. There was no laughter

in them. He had a long-jawed face slashed down the center
by a nose that resembled the prow of an outrigger canoe.
A pair of rustic black trousers were tucked into the tops of
high-heeled riding boots adorned with a pair of silver-
mounted spurs with long, curved shanks and huge silver-
dollar rowels that sang a chiming song each time the rider
moved his feet or his horse stepped sideways, restless to
be on the move.

He was seventy-one years of age and time had had its
way with him, but he was still dangerous and men who
remembered him from this mining camp or that one held
nothing but respect for the man called The Preacher.

For those who really knew him, and his uncanny speed
with the twin guns he wore, said his brand of preaching
was a great deal more effective than that offered by most
sky pilots.

He had returned now to Dead End to act as a referee in a
contest as unusual as any the West had ever known.

His orders were simple. Until the contest was over, no
man was to leave the canyon, and if one of the five
champions slated to match gun skills in this lonely town
lost his stomach for the game and tried to leave, The Preacher
would kill him, preferably from cover with a Winchester.

Chapter Two

Vent Torrey rode down the main street of Leadville, letting the big Appaloosa chose its own speed as he carefully examined each man he passed and each side street and alleyway. When he drew abreast of the city marshal's office, he pulled the horse in and sat looking at the door until a tall man wearing checkered pants, a brown shirt and buckskin vest emerged and leaned against a porch support chewing on a frayed match and gazing up at Vent.

Vent nodded slightly and said, "Marshal Bean. How are you?"

The marshal's thick face canted down as he watched a spider struggle to make it up onto the sidewalk, then, when it finally emerged on the boards of the walk, he calmly toed it into mush and, still looking down, said, "Fine as if I had good sense. . . . You?"

"Driftin'. Punched cows for the D-Diamond-B up on the Powder. Marshaled a spell at Winnemucca and rode shotgun for Wells Fargo outa Denver on the Cripple Creek run."

"Heard you shot a feller up at Miles City," Bean said.

Vent nodded. "Didn't give me no other way to go . . ."

"They seldom do," Bean agreed dryly. "Buy you a drink?"

Vent dismounted, tied the Appaloosa to the hitch rail and stepped up on the sidewalk, a tall, broad-shouldered young man with blunt features and brown eyes that missed nothing. His right thumb was hooked into a gun belt supporting a heavy .44 Colt pistol with grips worn smooth by much handling. However, it wasn't the gun that the marshal looked at but the hand itself.

Vent wore a peculiar leather contraption on the hand that almost completely hid the flesh with straps and buckles lacing the back and around the wrist.

"I never asked you why you wore that thing?" Bean said, and made it a question.

"Feller plugged me through the hand out in Kansas. Injun I got to know up near Crested Butte, a Ute, rigged it up for me. Without it, the hand's not worth much. With it . . ." and he let it go there, but Bean knew the rest of the story.

The Ute had named Vent Leatherhand and others took it up. Now the name meant dead men and a gun fast enough that some said Vent could beat the best, including John Hardin, Bill Longley, King Fisher and maybe even Wild Bill Hickok, the maniacal former army scout whose gun swiftness was legend and who was gunned down in Deadwood, South Dakota, in 1876.

No one really knew how many men this tall, young man with the cold eyes and confident manner had killed. Vent wasn't keeping score but some said he had put over twenty men down.

"Craig Bleeker's in town," Bean said suddenly.

Vent did not break stride. "He doing any talking?"

"Yep. Says he's gonna dust you on sight."

"Ummm . . ."

They turned into Pap Wyman's gambling palace on State and Harrison, and Vent, who had once been an assistant marshal in the town during its roaring birth pangs, found a lot of changes. The bar was lined with the usual conglomerate of miners, gamblers, cowboys and drifters, along with a number of buckskin-clad men, those solitary wanderers of far places, who, when they came to town, celebrated as if tomorrow would never come. They were quiet to the extreme, but Vent knew they could be as dangerous as a grizzly bear and as touchy when drunk. No man in his right mind interfered with them or their drinking unless it was at his own peril.

The marshal led the way to a table near the back of the room, nodding at a number of men as he passed the bar. Several drinkers glanced at Vent curiously but then turned back to their bottles when they caught his eye.

Sliding into chairs that placed their backs to the wall, Vent and the marshal had their careful look around the room, noting the tables crowded with gamblers taking up much of the center of the room and the two heavy-set bartenders wearing arm garters and sporting walrus mustaches.

One of them glanced up and, seeing Bean and his companion at the table, lifted a bottle from the ornate backbar, held it up and, when Bean nodded, brought it and two glasses to the table.

"Marshal, how's things?" the bartender asked, pouring each man a drink and leaving the bottle.

"Fine as frog's hair, Calley," Bean said, and then glanced at the front door as it swung wide, letting in a shaft of sunlight that splashed its light over the sawdust-strewn floor and winked out with the closing of the batwings.

"Damn!" he said, and Calley, looking over his shoulder, said softly, "Yonder comes trouble, marshal," and quickly returned to the backbar where he nudged his fellow bartender and nodded his head at the man who had just entered and was now standing three feet inside the room looking belligerently around.

Vent watched the newcomer with what appeared to be an almost complete lack of interest, but the moment the man entered the room, he had lowered his hand and removed the hammer thong from his gun.

"Well, so there's Bleeker," Bean said, and lifted his drink and drained it off and carefully poured another, held the bottle while Vent drank, then refilled his glass and set the jug to one side, not wanting it to obstruct his view.

Vent examined the gunman, noting the tied-down Smith and Wesson Russian .44 he wore. It was considered the most accurate pistol in the West at that time, but Vent did not like the curve of the handle, preferring the better-balanced Colts. Bleeker wore his weapon at hip level and slightly canted forward, a position Vent knew marked him as a professional. Turning to the marshal he said, "You know, Elam, I'm getting kinda tired of this sort of thing."

"Comes with the rep, Vent," Bean said, but he knew what Vent meant.

Bleeker stalked to the bar and men moved away, leaving him plenty of elbow room. Looking at Calley, the gunman said, "Whiskey, and leave the bottle," and when served he tilted the glass and drank it neat, then, spotting Vent in the backbar mirror, froze for a long moment, riveted his eyes on the man he had bragged he would kill on sight, lowered his glass and placed it gently on the bar and turned.

Vent watched him, waiting, then said quietly, "Elam, best find a neutral spot just in case this feller throws off."

Nodding, Bean rose and moved to the wall to the left of Vent, unhooked his hammer tiedown and waited, his eyes carefully logging the movements of the patrons, who had immediately sensed gunsmoke trouble and had begun to drift out of the line of fire.

"Not your put-in, Marshal," Bleeker said, not taking his eyes off Vent.

"I'm not in it," the marshal replied, adding coldly, "I'm here to make damn sure no one else buys in."

Bleeker smiled faintly and then raised a slow left hand and smoothed his handlebar mustache, tilted his hat back just a fraction and said, "Leatherhand, I told folks I planned to kill you on sight. Haven't changed my mind."

Vent mentally shrugged, remembering this man's brother in the cowtown far to the north lying in the dust where Vent had dropped him after an argument over a poker game. Now here was the big brother out to avenge his dead kin and Vent wondered where it would end. He was no stranger to feuds. His family and a family named Hawks had killed each other off for almost a hundred years, winding up in Missouri where they built their own private cemeteries with each other's victims. Now Vent was the last male Torrey and old man Hawks was all that remained of that family. Vent had no idea where the old man was, but could recall as if it were yesterday his final shoot-out with the family at a lonely Colorado railroad station back in the mountains. He had left two dead Hawkses and a gun-crippled old man and ridden away.

Looking at Bleeker, he wondered how many relatives

the man had and how many of them he would have to kill
before they gave up.

"Quit now while you're alive," Vent told Bleeker softly,
and watched the derision well up in the cold eyes and
thought, he thinks I'm afraid of him, and stood up.

"Damn you to hell!" Bleeker suddenly shouted and
dove for his gun.

Vent let him clear the sights of the .44, then shot him
through the body and watched the bit slug slam him gape-
mouthed against the bar, where he hung balanced delicately on his heels.

Starting at Vent, he let the gun slip back in its holster
and said distinctly, "Damn! You shot me clean through the
body. . . . God, it hurts like hell," and he stared down at
the swiftly spreading blanket of blood that was turning his
shirt red just below his heart.

"Sometimes a man dies learning," Vent told him bleakly.

Suddenly the gunman took a long step away from the
bar, his right hand clasping his wound, his left outstretched
in a futile gesture of protest, and said softly, "Oh, Lord
Jesus!" and then, eyes bulging in horror-filled wonder, his
knees quit on him and he crashed to the floor, causing the
bottles on the bar to execute a tiny jig.

Men around the room let out a collective sigh and one of
the bar girls began sobbing hysterically. Vent refilled his
glass, drained it and walked to the door and stepped into
the sunlight where he stood breathing deeply of the pure
mountain air. And as he stood there, he suddenly knew he
had to get away from towns and men looking to build their
reputations and men seeking revenge and men wanting to
hire his gun. At a sound behind him, he stepped clear of
the batwings and watched as four men carried the dead

gunman out onto the sidewalk and along the street toward the mortician's establishment.

Bean came out behind them, glanced at Vent and said, "He was a damn fool. You shaded him at least two seconds and still beat him all hollow."

"His brother wasn't any faster," Vent said, and then asked, "You suppose we could get something to eat without somebody wanting to shoot us up?"

"Let's go over to the Saddle Rock Café," Bean said, and led the way. Inside they sought a secluded corner and ordered two steaks, potates and gravy and biscuits so light it would take an ore car full to weigh a pound. Each man topped his order off with four eggs and, when the food arrived, dug in without preliminaries. The meal over, they ordered large slices of apple pie and washed them down with cups of steaming black coffee. Finished, they leaned back and lit up cigars ordered from the waitress and Bean said, "Hope ya got time to hang around for the inquest."

"When'll that be?" Vent asked.

"In about an hour," Bean said, and grinned.

The inquest was over quickly. Bean, Calley, the bartender and his assistant testified that Bleeker had drawn first and had instigated the fight.

Said the coroner, a crusty individual with a flowing beard, a stovepipe hat and long black coat that he wore buttoned up to his chin, "The victim, one Craig Bleeker, met death at the hands of one, what's yere given name, son?" and when Vent told him, continued, "met death at the hands of one Vent Torrey, known as Leatherhand. I hearby rule that Mr. Torrey fired in defense of his life and that Bleeker died of a bullet from Mr. Torrey's gun. He, said Bleeker, also died, in this court's estimation, of damn foolishness. Case closed. Mr. Torrey, you are free to go," and the gavel came down, emptying the room of spectators, who, satisfied with the official ruling, repaired to the nearest bar for drinks.

As Bean and Vent stepped into the street, a man carrying a Winchester rifle under one arm nodded at Bean, then said, "Mr. Torrey, my name's Gig Bates. I work for Stiles Burlingame-Leach. I'd like a word with you."

Vent had heard, as anyone living in the West at that time for more than a month had heard, about Leach and his silver empire.

"If he's looking for a gun, I'm not for hire," Vent said shortly.

"He's not looking to hire you," Bates said. "But I think you better listen to what I've got to say. It concerns your sister, Rhonda."

Vent turned eyes resembling the twin bores of a shotgun on Bates and asked softly, "She's all right, ain't she?"

"She's all right," Bates assured him.

"Then let's talk," Vent said, and, nodding at Bean, turned and led Bates toward where his horse was tied.

They sat on a long bench in front of the marshal's office and Vent carefully examined Bates, who appeared nondescript and unassuming. He did not carry a handgun unless he had one concealed on his body somewhere, but the rifle seemed as if it were part of him. Many men in the West preferred a rifle, Vent knew, having failed to master a handgun. Tom Horn, the gunman and former army scout, was a good example. He seldom ever carried a handgun, but his aim and skill with the rifle he habitually toted was legend.

"What's this about my sister?" Vent asked, carefully rolling a cigarette.

Bates looked across the street, seemingly engrossed in a

man loading a wagon with sacks of grain, then said quietly, "She's been kidnapped, Mr. Torrey," and waited.

Vent sat still for a long moment, then looking at Bates, who refused to meet his eyes, said quietly, "If you had anything to do with this, mister, you're a dead man walking."

Bates turned then and shook his head. "I'm only a messenger. I work for Leach. He sent me to tell you he has your sister and they's just one way you can get her released."

"Why?" Vent asked.

Bates shrugged. "It's some damn fool bet he made with some other fellers he gambles with. You ever hear of Tombstone Morgan . . . or Amos Dewberry . . . or Deak Hammer . . . or maybe Jake Sunderman?"

"All big ranchers, miners and moneymen," Vent said. "Yeah, I've heard of them."

"Well, they made this here bet. They each picked out a pistol fighter to back and bet ten thousand dollars on him. You were Leach's choice."

"To do what?" Vent asked, and deep inside he felt the slow coil of a savage anger that was rising ever closer to the surface. He knew that if Bates said the wrong thing, he would kill him.

"I'm supposed to tell you to go to a ghost town called Dead End up in the Medicine Bow Mountains. You'll find four other fellers there. The rules of the bet are that each one of you fellers must try and kill the others. The man left will get twenty-five thousand dollars and the bettor whose gunfighter wins gets fifty thousand."

Vent stared at him. "You mean these here big shots are betting on who'll wind up killing the rest. Man, they must be loco."

Bates shook his head. "Nope, Mr. Torrey, just bored. Me, I don't hold with this kinda thing. It goes against everything I believe in. I've put my share of fellers in the ground, but they was fair standup fights and I won because I was the faster, but this . . ."

"So they got Rhonda?" and Vent knew that before this thing was over Leach would die.

"They picked her up just out of Crested Butte coming back from town," Bates said.

"What about her man?"

"He knows. I've had my talk with him," and Bates fingered a slight swelling on the left side of his jaw, observing, "He's sure as hell got a flash temper."

"You're lucky he didn't kill you," Vent said.

"I guessed that," Bates said.

Tossing his burned away cigarette into the dust of the street, Vent absently watched a tall rider on a beautiful black horse trot into the head of Harrison and pull his animal down to a walk. The man looked familiar.

"Who else will be at Dead End?" Vent asked.

"Slab Borden, Angel Augustino, Coup Arbuckle, Owney Sharp and you," Bates told him, then, looking up as the man on the black horse neared the marshal's office, said mildly, "Looks like Owney Sharp's been approached."

Sharp stopped his horse in front of the marshal's office and, carefully removing a cigar from the pocket of his vest, shot the sleeves of his ruffled white shirt. Cutting the end off the smoke with a small gold pen knife, he put it between his mobile lips, fired it up and grinned at Vent around a cloud of smoke right out of Havana.

"I hear they've turned you into a gambler, Mr. Torrey," he said.

Vent nodded. "How'd they rope you in?"

"Bought out my paw's mortgage. He stands to lose everything if I don't cooperate."

"Who's your sponsor?" Vent asked.

"Amos Dewberry," Sharp growled, and the sound came out like broken chunks of rock falling down a well.

"Why don't we just go kill all five of these fellers?" Vent asked.

"Not a bad idea," Sharp agreed, and watched Bates.

"Won't work, boys, not unless you plan to go to Europe. All five of your sponsors lit a shuck outa the States as soon as the bet went down. They left the particulars to fellers like me. Won't do no good to plug me. Like I told you, I'm just an errand boy."

"You, Mr. Bates, are in a dirty business," Sharp said, leveling gimlet eyes on the man.

"You know who's going to be there?" Vent asked Sharp.

Sharp grinned. "The hunchback for one. Slab Borden for another. The Mex, Augustino. He's being sponsored by Tombstone Morgn."

"Looks like they got us roped and hogtied," Vent said, and turned and asked Bates, "When's this here shindig supposed to get under way?"

"July third," Bates said. "Until then nobody fires a shot. If the pledge is broken, the man that breaks it will die."

Sharp stared at him. "The hell ya say? Whose gonna kill him?"

Bates grinned sourly. "You ever hear of a feller named The Preacher?"

Both Vent and Sharp stared at him, then Sharp said, "I'll be damned. I thought he was long dead."

"Nope," Bates said. "He's alive and still shooting. In

fact, he's the referee in this here waltz. He usta be marshal of Dead End. Knows the country. He'll be close by. Anyone violates the rules, he's got orders to put a .50 Sharps slug through the feller's brisket. Anyone tries to leave, he gets the same medicine.''

''Thought of everything, didn't they?'' Sharp said disgustedly.

''What'll stop the survivor from hunting up these moneymen after the dancing's all over and dusting them down?'' Vent asked.

Bates shook his head. ''They thought of that too. The survivor comes hunting them, he'll find himself up against half a dozen shooters. They made a deal with Billy Krebs, Killing Jim Miller and a couple of others, including Tonto McCord, who works for Sunderman, to protect them.''

''I didn't think Krebs would be a party to this kind of thing,'' Vent said.

''Hell, he loves a good gamble just like everybody else does,'' Bates grunted, and Vent knew he was right. All over the West people would be choosing sides and placing bets. If you can't do anything about it, ride along with it, he told himself and rose and walked to his horse and mounted, looked at Sharp and said, ''Care to ride along with me?''

''My pleasure, pard,'' Sharp said, and the two rode north toward Dead End and Arapahoe country.

Chapter Three

Coup Arbuckle cursed the big black stud he rode as the animal shied from a rattler lying coiled on a rock by the side of the trail, buzzing signal flag quivering above its body, its head weaving back and forth, tiny tongue licking out and back, bringing the odor of danger to the creature.

Arbuckle's left hand dropped and rose with uncanny speed, his fist suddenly filled with the bulk of a .45 and the snake lost its head. The man with the hunchback shrugged the serape he wore to conceal his abnormality further around his shoulders, punched out the spent shell and carefully reloaded, leaving the snake's body twisting beside the rock.

Coup Arbuckle didn't give a damn about anything. He had ridden with Quantrill's raiders down in the Missouri breaks and later with the outlaw King Fisher, whose fearsome reputation was almost unequaled in the West at that time.

The hunchback's affliction tore at him like a broken boil

and, knowing he would never be like other men, he set out at the age of sixteen to prove he was as good as they were. His right hand hung deformed at his side, useless for anything more than, as he often said with twisted sarcasm, "a way to balance my body so it don't fall over to the left."

But his left hand possessed a skill all its own. It could conjure up a gun as if by magic, and during a twelve-year career in which Arbuckle sold his gun to the highest bidder, he had killed twenty-six men. Unlike the swaggering saloon bravos and dime-novel gunfighters, he counted Mexicans and Indians.

"Anybody that thinks a 'Pache ain't a match for a white man will soon find hisself staked out on an anthill," he said, and so he counted Indians. He had the same sort of respect for Mexicans because he did not kill peons. The fights he had were with gunfighters like himself.

Now he rode his big stud toward the ghost town of Dead End, his half-crazed eyes missing nothing as he effortlessly controlled the horse, who was as vicious as its master. Arbuckle's mouth was a bitter cut in a flat face bisected by a Roman nose. He had almost no eyebrows and his hair was a dirty yellow and stuck out in tufts from beneath a battered Stetson hat. His five-foot nine-inch frame was carelessly dressed in a pair of dark brown pants, a blue shirt and high-topped boots adorned with California spurs, heavy laden with silver. He wore his gun belt lower than most men in his profession. The worn .45 was thrust into a cut-away holster butt outward, a deception that had cost a number of men their lives.

He wore his gun in that position so that men would believe he favored a cross draw. Not knowing he couldn't use his right hand, they watched the hand for that first telltale movement and died as he drew left-handed, twisting the weapon out and away from his body. It was a method mastered by Bill Hickok, but where the famous marshal wore two guns, Arbuckle wore one.

He had also mastered the ability to load and fire a Winchester with his left hand, no mean feat in itself.

Now he put the stud to the slope leading into the canyon where the town of Dead End lay hidden from the world, and thought about this strange gamble he had become a part of. He had not balked. Nor was he startled by the idea of five men deliberately pitting themselves against each other for a huge dollar pot, winner take all. When Tonto McCord came to him in Dodge City and made him Sunderman's offer, he had coolly examined the gunfighter and then asked, "How come Sunderman don't send you?"

McCord had grinned and said in his gravelly voice, "He didn't think I was fast enough to compete."

"Do you?"

"Nope."

It was the hunchback's turn to grin. "Know your limits, do you?"

"That's a true story," McCord said. "The band plays its first waltz on July third and the rules are that nobody fires a gun before sunup on that day."

"What if one of us decides to break the rule?" Arbuckle asked curiously.

"Then there is no payoff and The Preacher pops a buffalo gun whistler through yore think box."

"The Preacher? Hell, I thought he was dead and long in the ground," Arbuckle said with surprise.

"Nope, he's still alive and kicking. He works for the men who set this up and Arbuckle, he's as good as he always was," McCord warned.

"Heard of him," Arbuckle said shortly, then nodded,

tossed off his drink and said, "It's a long ride to Dead End
. . . Dead End . . . hell of a name, that," and he walked
out of the saloon where they had met, mounted the stud,
who squealed and tried to buck him off and failing that,
reached back and attempted to bite a chunk out of the
hunchback's knee and received a kick in the nose for his
efforts.

Now the big animal took the grade into the main street
of Dead End almost effortlessly, stopping at the south end
of town when Arbuckle reined him in. Sitting there, the
hunchback had his look, cataloging each building for fu-
ture reference, memorizing the general layout of the town,
then glancing up at the cemetery, thought, more folks
buried there than this place ever held, and gigged his horse
and rode boldly down Main Street, the dust rising in small
puffs from beneath the stud's hooves.

Watching his approach from a push-backed chair on the
verandah of the hotel, Angel Augustino rolled the thin
Mexican cigar in his teeth and spat into the dust, the spittle
leaving a small island of wetness in a blanket of dryness.

Augustino loved clothes. He favored black Mexican pants
with accentuated bell bottoms and silver stitching up the
outside of each leg. His boots were bench-made and adorned
with butterfly stitching. Huge Mexican spurs, favored by
many men in the West, hung from his bootheels, a tiny set
of bells giving off a musical sound each time he moved.
His shirt was wine red and fit his broad shoulders perfectly.
A silver decorated vest completed the ensemble. On top of
his mop of curly hair he wore a large Mexican sombrero
with tiny cloth balls dangling from strings around its brim
and a rattlesnake headband around the crown, the rattles
still in place. His slim hips were resting places for a pair of
twin .45 Colts, their frames covered with scrollwork and

the butt plates made from staghorn. The holsters and cartridge belt were also covered with silverwork.

Augustino was a man who smiled. He smiled when he killed a man and he smiled when he drank his beloved tequila. He had once been known to skin a man alive with the deadly little stiletto he carried in a sheath down the back of his neck and smiled all during the ghastly procedure. Women adored his dark, aquiline features and great brown eyes. He looked like an aristocrat and so he was, having come down from a long line of extremely wealthy Mexican ranchers whose descendants still controlled vast tracts of grazing land south of the border.

The Mexican had smiled his way through twenty-two killings and now, as Arbuckle pulled his horse to a stop in the street, Augustino tipped his hat back, smiled at the hunchback and said, *"Como lo haré, cazador?"*

Arbuckle, like many men of the West, spoke and understood Spanish. He looked at the Mexican sourly and said, *"Estoy seco. Cerveza?"*

"No beer, my friend, I must apologize for our host's obvious shortsightedness. I guess you'll just have to stay dry or drink from the stream."

"Damn," Arbuckle grunted, and turned and rode toward the creek, ignoring the Mexican.

Watching him ride off, Augustino grinned.

Arbuckle had his drink, then put the stud in one of the corrals on the east bank of the water course and watched as the big animal promptly kicked half a dozen corral poles into kindling and then stepped delicately over the wreckage and walked to a grassy bank and began eating, unconcernedly ignoring its master. Cursing, Arbuckle walked back across the creek on a shaky footbridge that led to the back door of the blacksmith shop and emerged into the street just as a huge bear of a man riding an ugly black mule came up over the rise south of town and trotted into the main street, staying clear of the railroad track.

Slab Borden rode hunched over, his body sagging at an awkward angle as the mule grunted under the load of his 240-pound frame. His long arms dangled loosely at his sides as he allowed the mule its head, knowing it would seek the creek first. To the casual observer, it would appear that the big man was uninterested in anything around him, but just the opposite was true. He missed nothing as the mule trotted along Main Street, then turned between two buildings and down to the creek, immediately dipping its nose deep in the cool water. Borden slid off its back, lifted a canteen from around the saddle horn and knelt, rinsed it out and refilled it with the sweet water of the stream. As he raised the canteen and drank from it, he looked along the alley, saw Augustino sitting in a chair in front of the hotel and lowered it, brushed away the loose water from his face with a dirty sleeve and pulled the saddle from the mule. He heaved it effortlessly to his left shoulder, left the mule there, marched back to the main street, crossed it and stopped in front of the hotel.

He stood there, a giant man with a perpetual scowl on his blunt face, his shoe-button eyes peering out at a world he hated, and said nothing.

Borden's reputation had been built on the phenomenon of his terrible strength. He had killed eleven men, two of them by simply bending them across his knee until their backs cracked, and the other nine by blasting them into infinity with the sawed-off shotgun he wore on his right hip in a specially constructed swivel holster. In a gunfight, Borden merely spun the weapon and holster on the swivel pin and cut loose with both barrels. Such a weapon at forty feet could lay an entire street full of men bare. It was a fearsome machine with devastating potential in the right hands. Borden knew how to use it to its best advantage.

Looking at the Mexican, he asked, "Who's here?"

Nodding toward the inside of the hotel, Augustino said, "The hunchback is inside. He plays solitary and cheats himself."

"Any whiskey around?"

"No whiskey, señor. Only water," Augustino said.

"What about grub?"

"Plenty. Our hosts have provided only the best. It's in the hotel kitchen. There are also five rooms upstairs provided with all the comforts of home, if a man had a home."

"What's that supposed to mean?" Borden asked, his eyes vicious in their intensity.

"Nothing, *amigo*. I was speaking of myself. I do not have a home and do not want one."

Borden grunted and trudged up the steps and across the wooden sidewalk while Augustino watched the boards bend beneath the man's weight.

"Welcome to Dead End and the lottery of death," Augustino called after the retreating figure, and chuckled.

Borden ignored him. Inside the hotel he found Arbuckle sitting alone at a table, a game of solitary spread before him.

"Nice of you to show up for your funeral," Borden said, staring at the hunchback.

Arbuckle did not look up. "On July fourth, I will celebrate your death by using your grave for a toilet," he said, placing a black queen on a black king.

"Still cheating at solitary, I see," Borden said.

"I cheat at poker too, but nobody ever calls me," the hunchback countered.

"Maybe we can have a poker game July third," Borden suggested.

"Good idea," Arbuckle replied, and then looked up and started at the huge man. Borden, gazing back into the half-crazed eyes, was not intimidated.

After he had taken the stairs two at a time and disappeared along the hall, the hunchback snarled, "Son of a bastard," and went back to his card game.

Far to the south, two men squatted around a small campfire and ate silently from tin plates.

Vent Torrey had decided he was not going to become a part of any man's game unless he himself chose to do so. It went against everything he believed in to allow other men to move him around the board of life at a whim, but how to stop this thing was the problem. Half the allotted time had passed and they were still four days from Dead End. Vent had no idea what would happen if he failed to keep his date with destiny. He did not believe Leach would have his sister murdered in cold blood. On the other hand, it was a risk he was not willing to take.

Glancing at his companion he said, "Owney, I ain't going through with this."

The gambler looked up, took another bite of beans and said, "Just what I was thinking. It sorta goes against the grain to let a man dictate to me how I'm gonna die. If I gotta check out, I'd prefer I put myself in harm's way rather than some damn big money gambler looking for a new thrill."

"Question is, how we gonna beat these fellers at their own game?"

Vent thought about it for a long minute, then it came to him. Gunfighters were a special breed. They held great respect for each other's expertise and very seldom, if ever, went to war with each other. The odds were long that both shooters would wind up on boothill. When they met, they usually bought each other a drink, then moved on. The West was a big place and men of the gunfighting fraternity did not like to share territory. Each worked his own side of the street and if the wanderers, such as Vent Torrey, rode into the bailiwick of another gunfighter, he usually passed the time of day and moved on. And when these men did come together, it was more than likely for a cause.

Thinking about it, Vent recalled a recent incident in which Luke Short was ordered out of Dodge, and within days the train pulled into the station and off stepped a dozen of the West's top gunmen. There was no fight and Short stayed in Dodge as the pistoleers, having accomplished their mission without firing a shot, quietly reboarded the train and left town.

Setting his plate to one side, he rolled a cigarette, fired it up and said musingly, "I wonder how they managed to get Arbuckle and the Mexican to agree to this?"

"And Slab Borden. Hell, he's as indpendent as a Siwash bronc."

"With the Mex it would be the excitement," Vent guessed.

"And the hunchback would go into it because of curiosity," Sharp said. "I know him and he's a man to wonder whether he could win such a bet and would be willing to risk his life on it."

Vent nodded. "Borden probably wants the money. I heard he once killed a feller for a two-dollar knife."

"He's also the best horsethief this side the Missouri," Sharp added.

"We could probably swing that damn hunchback over if we got him mad enough at that bunch of moneymakers."

"I think I could talk Augustino into coming over," Sharp said. "Me and him, we did a little thing together down in Texas. Saved his butt for him. He kinda owes me."

"Then we either gotta find a way to guarantee more money for Borden than he could make if he won, or kill the man," Vent said.

"You got a plan?"

Vent nodded, tossed his used-up cigarette into the flames and rose and gathered an armload of wood to feed the fire, then said, "First, we get my sis loose. Next step is to find where these fellers are vulnerable and hit them there until they're forced to come back and protect their interests."

Sharp was beginning to catch on. "Neat, very neat. We tear down fences, run off cattle, blow up mines, rob their damn banks and run off their men until they come back, then we go after them."

Vent's eyes were cold and depthless as he said, "That's it exactly, but I've got a special plan for those fellers."

"Oh?"

"I'll put it to you when I've got it all worked out," Vent said.

"What about The Preacher?" Sharp asked. He had forgotten all about that grim specter out of the past.

"We'll trap the fox, then make him a deal." Vent grinned and crawled into his bedroll while Sharp checked the horses and stoked up the fire. "I'll take first watch," he said, and moved into the night like a black-garbed ghost.

*   *   *

The man called The Preacher crouched over a smokeless fire in a narrow crack in the rocks high above the town of Dead End and sipped his coffee. Near to hand, a heavy Sharps rifle lay against a rock and two six-shooters swung at his hips.

As he lifted the cup for another sip, a man stepped into view at the narrow aperture leading to the Preacher's refuge, pushed back his hat with a leather-covered right hand and said quietly, "Howdy, Preacher. Heard you was dead. Must have been gossip, or you're walking around to save burial expenses."

"You're pretty quiet, Leatherhand," the black-garbed man said, lifting his grizzled head and staring at Vent from beneath snow-white eyebrows. His eyes, Vent noted, were as sharply blue as if he were twenty years old and the hand, the left one, that held the coffee cup, was as steady as an iron bar.

"My friend Owney Sharp is up above you there with his rifle sights laid on your backbone," Vent said conversationally.

"Umm . . . gonna kill me?"

"Nope. Just want to palaver. You willing?"

"Come and set," The Preacher invited, and moved over to give Vent room, offering him the half-filled coffee cup as the Missourian crouched against the rock wall.

Vent accepted the cup and, looking up to where Owney leaned against a boulder twenty feet above the fire, asked, "Any reason for leaving Owney up there?"

The Preacher grinned frostily. "No, I ain't lived this long from being stupid. I know I can't shade either one of you boys. Might have twenty years ago, but even then, I reckon they's a good chance we both would have gone down.''

Owney disappeared from his perch and, as the men sat silently waiting, made his way down the cliff and strolled into the cul-de-sac and settled on his haunches near the fire, his eyes on the entrance way.

''This box make you nervous?'' The Preacher asked, and there was a gleam in his eye as he put the question.

Sharp nodded.

''Preacher, I ain't a feller to pound around a thing. Believe in getting right to the guts. These old boys you work for took my sister. They bought Owney's father's mortgage. Now, me, I don't plan to do what they want and neither does Owney. They know better than to kill or harm my sister . . .''

The Preacher, looking into Vent's eyes, saw something there that made him wish he hadn't become a part of this. ''So, what's you boys' plan?''

''First things first,'' Sharp said mildly. ''We want your word you'll back off. We'll match your fee and let you keep on living and that's a fair bargain.''

The Preacher looked at the fire for a long moment, then looked up and said, ''The threat of dyin' don't bother me. Hell, me, I been dyin' for years. It's just that nobody's bothered to shovel the dirt in. I never went against a man who hired me, even for more money, but I don't hold with kidnapping an innocent girl. They told me all you boys were in favor of this match. They said you was going for the money.''

Looking up at Vent then, he added, ''I'd heard you weren't that kinda man, Leatherhand. I should have remembered that and looked a little closer at the hole card.''

''I'm not that kind of man. I don't fight men for fun or

profit," Vent said. "I've never hired my gun. I've been in range wars. Fought in one in Montana. When it was over, I drew puncher's wages and rode out. Just because a bunch of highbinders want a new gambling thrill doesn't mean I'll be a part of it."

"What you gonna do?" The Preacher asked, looking at the two men keenly.

"You out of it?" Sharp asked.

"Hell, not only am I out, but I might just join you fellers. I don't like a man lying to me, and these boys lied," The Preacher said, and his voice suddenly turned cold and hard and Vent knew how this old gunfighter had stayed alive so long.

"All right, your word suits me, Owney?"

"I'll take his word anytime," Sharp said. "Hell, he's a preacher, ain't he?"

"I usta be," the man in black said, and grinned.

"Good enough," Vent told him, and stood up and walked to where he could look down into Dead End. "We're going to convince those fellers down there to come over on our side, then we're going to ride through some moneymen's flower gardens and see if we can't bring them to the front door."

The Preacher began to smile as he saw where Vent was heading. "Hell, that sounds like fun. Besides, me, I'm getting stale just drifting around from poker game to poker game."

Owney looked at him sharply, then said, "Come to think about it, I heard you was one hell of a poker player in your day."

"Still am," The Preacher said, and rose, and, looking at

his new partners, nodded toward the valley and suggested, "Shall we ride down there?"

They retrieved their horses and rode down the trail to Dead End.

Chapter Four

Slab Borden sat on the front steps of the Dead End Hotel and whittled on a piece of wood with a huge bowie knife. Each time he drew the wicked blade along the piece of pine, a large shaving fell away and fluttered into the dust.

Sitting in his chair, Angel Augustino leaned against the wall of the building, boots crossed at the ankle and spurs hooked over the porch rail. His hat was pulled low, revealing a pair of alert brown eyes that missed nothing.

As the two sat wordlessly, the hunchback came out, walked to the edge of the verandah and had his quick look at the empty town, then glanced down canyon and grunted. "Riders comin'," he said, and brushed the serape back, clearing his gun butt. Deftly he slipped the tiedown from the hammer and waited stolidly.

Borden looked up, gazed a moment downtrail, then glanced back at Arbuckle and said sharply, "Don't stand behind me, feller. It makes me nervous."

Arbuckle chuckled. "Afraid I'll drill ya in the back?" he asked mockingly.

"Don't you wish?" Borden snarled. Arbuckle moved further along the verandah and, leaning a shoulder against a porch support, watched the oncoming riders.

Augustino remained motionless, his hands crossed limply in his lap.

As The Preacher and Sharp, looking like twin circuit-riding ministers in their funeral black garb, rode into the main street sided by Vent Torrey on the Appaloosa, Arbuckle observed softly, "Two black crows and an eagle."

Borden watched them come on until they pulled their horses in before the hotel, then tossed the whittling stick into the dirt and stood up. "More little lambs to the slaughter," he grunted.

"Ah, *amigos*, welcome to Dead End, the land of opportunity, the abode of yesterday's ghosts and tomorrow's hopes," the Mexican said, and rose languorously, stretched and catwalked to the rail and, placing both hands on it, grinned widely.

Sharp looked at Vent and then asked The Preacher, "These the fellers we're supposed to bump off?"

The Preacher nodded. "That's them, ready and waiting."

"Don't look like much," Sharp observed.

"You can break leather and find out," Arbuckle invited.

Vent smiled and, glancing at Sharp, said, "This here feller has a neat trick. He makes out like he's going for his iron with his right hand then ups and cuts loose with his left in a Hickok backhand draw. Nails the other feller while he's watching that right hand. Pretty sneaky, huh?"

Sharp shook his head. "Not bad, but it could get a man killed if the other gent don't fall for it."

Arbuckle grinned. "I hear you can't do a damn thing

without the leather contraption on your hand. That right, Torrey?''

"Don't ever test it," Vent said, and his eyes were as emotionless as a dead man's.

"Hell, I don't plan to. I'll just let old Slab here cut you in half with that scattergun he totes," the hunchback said maliciously.

"Mean little bastard, ain't he?" Sharp said.

Vent looked at the three for a moment, then nodded at Augustino and asked, "How come you're in this shindig, Angel? I heard you were a man who fought because he enjoyed it. Dollar need finally catch up to you?"

"One gets bored, no?"

Sharp smiled and observed, "In this kind of game, a man could get bored to death."

Vent nodded and turned his horse and rode to the creek. The others followed. After their horses drank their fill and the men had washed their faces in the sweet water and also drank, the horses were led across the stream and up the bank where they were carefully staked out in the deep green grass. The stud came over boldly and sniffed Sharp's horse's nose, squealed and whirled and kicked at him, only to receive a resounding kick in return. Not liking the reception, the big brute went away and began feeding again.

As Vent and his companions walked across Main Street carrying their saddlebags and Winchesters, Sharp told Arbuckle, "That's a mean damn animal you got over there."

"Ain't he a dandy?" the hunchback said, and led the way into the hotel. The Mexican and Borden followed along and the men sat down around a dust-covered poker table.

Vent, carefully sizing them up, asked, "You boys set on this game?"

Arbuckle, who was probably as smart as the Mexican, carefully examined The Preacher's face, then observed, "I figure something's come up different what with The Preacher here down off his perch and walking among us."

Vent looked straight at Arbuckle and said quietly, "I came here because they kidnapped my sister. This ain't my kind of game, and I figure you boys know that. Sharp, he don't play these games either, but they bought up his paw's mortgage and unless Owney goes along, they foreclose and toss the old man off his ranch. He's eighty-two years old."

Borden grunted sourly.

The Mexican pushed his hat back and smiled.

Arbuckle thought about it for a moment, then said, "I wondered how they got you boys roped in," then, nodding at The Preacher, asked, "What's his game?"

"He's siding us," Vent said.

Augustino smiled and, looking around, observed, "Here we sit, some of the best in this part of the West, and we're letting men deal us the cards and tell us how to play them, and the pot is death. *Amigos*, I am not fool enough to believe that one of us could kill another without taking some lead in return. The chances are excellent that we will all die."

"Yep, I agree," Vent said.

"So, you have a plan and that plan does not involve shooting each other. Right, *amigo*?"

Vent grinned. "We have a plan, but we need you fellers to make it work."

Slab Borden looked up and growled, "What's in it for us?"

"More than you'll make trying to plug one of us and a damn sight less dangerous," Sharp said.

Arbuckle shook his head. "I made a deal. I don't back down."

Vent looked at him for a moment, then stood up, walked to the bar, turned and said softly, "Draw," and suddenly Arbuckle was looking down the dealy bore of Vent's .44.

"Hey, what the hell?" the hunchback protested.

Borden and the Mexican remained seated, carefully keeping their hands on the table.

"I could blow you out of that chair and end this talk, but that's not why I came to Dead End. I came to get you fellers to side me."

"For a man asking help, you're pretty damn sudden there," Borden, apparently unruffled by Vent's gun work, observed dryly.

"Just a lesson," Vent said. "There isn't a man among you that can beat me, but I don't kill for fun or money." He holstered his gun and came and sat back down, keeping a wary eye on the hunchback, who was quite obviously toying with the idea of drawing on him.

"I wouldn't if I were you," Sharp warned.

"Good advice, *amigo*," Augustino agreed. "Let us listen to the man with the leather hand. He intrigues me."

"How about you, Borden? You willing to listen?" Vent asked, watching the big man who was always an enigma. Vent knew Borden might go along, then again, he might come up blasting with the scattergun he wore and the Missourian guessed that even if he put six slugs in the giant, the man would still get off both barrels of the shotgun and somebody would die.

For a long moment, Borden looked at the dusty tabletop, then he met Vent's eyes and said, "You guarantee we'll make as much as we would if we went through with this and won, and I'm your man.''

"How many cattle would you need to make enough to match the combine's promise?'' Vent asked, watching Borden's face.

"About 2,500 head and they'd have to be prime,'' Borden replied, without thinking it over.

"You got a market?'' Vent asked.

Borden grinned sourly. "I got a dozen markets. Cows and horses, but more places to get rid of horses than cows.''

"There's plenty of horses where the cows are coming from,'' Vent assured him.

Arbuckle cocked his head and asked, "What you got in mind?''

"First, we get my sister back. After that, we pick up enough money to clear old man Sharp's mortgage. Then we start dismantling five empires.''

Borden stared at him. "You mean you plan to go after Jake Sunderman and his crowd?''

"That's exactly what I plan to do,'' Vent said, watching their faces as they rolled it over in their minds. He knew the idea would be just wild enough to appeal to such men, men who he also knew had stayed alive because they each had a streak of caution in their makeup. He was certain each man had a plan worked out that would have given him the edge if the five-way duel had been carried through. Vent had no intention of allowing that to happen, if he had to kill all three of these men where they sat.

Arbuckle looked long and intently at Vent and Vent knew the man was trying to read him. Finally Arbuckle glanced out the door at the dusty street and said softly, "Me, I think it would be one hell of a shindig. I kinda like the idea of turning the aces back to back on these money boys.''

Inwardly Vent sighed and told himself, that's one. Now for the other two. ''How about you, Borden? You along, or is this too tough a bronc for you to ride?''

''I'm in, but if the money ain't there, you better kill me, because if you don't, I'm gonna dust you for damn sure,'' Borden threatened.

''Just so,'' Vent agreed, and watched Augustino wordlessly.

The Mexican, still wearing his smile, shrugged eloquently, rose and walked to the bar, then turned and said, ''I think maybe what you plan to do would please me more than shooting at you. I also understand men such as Sunderman and his friends. We have the same *cabrones* in Mexico. I will play this game because it amuses me to turn—how you say, the tables—on these men.''

The six gunmen slept at Dead End that night, ate a quick breakfast the following morning and rode down canyon, leaving the old ghost town behind.

As they trotted from the main street, Vent looked back and for just a second thought he saw a shadowy form slip down an alley, but then passed it off as a trick of the shifting early-morning sun and turned and faced the downtrail.

The sun had reached its zenith when the six gunmen rode into the main street of Crested Butte. Several sidewalk loungers stared at them as they passed, their eyes speculative. Opposite the marshal's office they drew rein as a middle-aged man wearing a star stepped onto the sidewalk and, hands on hips, surveyed the horsemen.

''Gentlemen, I'm Marshal Ed Crank, the man who's

supposed to keep the peace in this here shebang,'' he said, and Vent had his look and saw a white-haired, spare-framed man with faded blue eyes radiating smile lines. He had a tough, mobile mouth and chin that promised determination. His long-fingered hands were hooked into a heavy cartridge belt that sagged around his waist, supporting a .45 Colt in a cutaway holster. He was dressed like a range rider, in Levi's, runover boots and a battered Stetson pushed to the back of his head.

Vent nodded solemnly and said, ''We are not in your town to cause you trouble, Marshal, or any other man, for that matter. We are just passing through, planning a visit to Lost Lake, where my sister has a small ranch.''

The marshal let his eyes wander from man to man, then observed dryly, ''I hope your sister has a strong constitution. You fellers would scare hell outa a cavalry regiment.''

Augustino smiled. ''We are very good fellows, very law-abiding, Marshal,'' he said.

Crank smiled frostily and replied, ''Well, Mr. Angel Augustino, it just so happens I ain't got a flyer on you, but I can't say the same for a couple of your friends.''

Ignoring the sally, Vent asked, ''Charlie Brady up at Lost Lake?''

''He was a week ago,'' Crank said.

''Thanks, Marshal.'' Vent nodded. ''We'll eat, have us a drink or two, get a night's rest and maybe even a bath, and move out in the morning.''

''Have at her. Me, I ain't paid to interfere with honest fellers traveling through the country,'' Crank said, and waving a negligent hand, reentered his office and quietly closed the door.

Vent clucked at the Appaloosa and rode to the Chinaman's Chance Café, where he rounded at the hitch rack, dismounted and led his companions inside. They took a long table against a wall and sat facing the door.

The owner stared at his customers in consternation, then came hurriedly around the counter to the table. "What'll it be, gents? Got some fresh beef, or I can give you mountain-caught trout. I've even got some fresh-raised strawberries."

They ordered steak and potatoes and a large pot of black coffee. When the meal came, they ate wordlessly while the proprietor kept staring at them.

Halfway through the meal, several riders, just off the range, came pushing through the front door, kidding and jostling each other. When they saw the six gun-hung men at the back table, they stopped and suddenly were silent. Vent watched them and saw pride work its way and knew they wouldn't leave the room no matter how much the gunfighters might intimidate them. He was right. They sought out tables, ordered loudly and took up their kidding, and Vent suddenly wondered what it would be like to be that free and easy. To be able to enter a saloon or reastaurant, or just ride down a street without having to watch one's back every moment, would be sheer pleasure. The only place he had found he could do this was high in some mountain meadow or lost canyon far from the haunts of men, and even then old habits would not go away. Not liking his thoughts, he finished his meal, drank a third cup of coffee and stood up, dropped money on the table and led the gunmen from the restaurant. As they passed out the door, Vent heard the sudden clamor of voices as the cowboys inside began speculating out loud as to who they were.

Standing on the sidewalk, they looked along Main Street, checked each side street, alleyway, window and rooftop, then untied their horses and led them across the street, retied them in front of the Sundance Palace, and pushed inside, stopping just beyond the door to let their eyes adjust to the dimness. Voices suddenly stilled as several patrons looked up from the bar and five men playing poker swiveled their heads and took inventory of the gunmen.

The men moved to two tables at the back of the room, sat down and waited until the bartender came over. Vent said, "Two bottles and six glasses and leave them, friend."

When the liquor came, each man had his first drink and Vent watched them as one by one they filled their glasses, lifted them and let the hot fluid slide down their throats. He did not worry about any of them getting drunk. Men like these could not afford to drink too much, he knew. To do so was inviting death. A drunk man was anybody's victim and to men who had left enemies by the dozens on their backtrail, it was wise to stay sober and alert.

Borden drank three drinks, then sat fondling his glass broodingly.

The hunchback, his eyes pinned on a red-haired saloon girl standing near the end of the bar, slowly sipped his whiskey, then, when the girl glanced at him, motioned. Reluctantly, she came over.

Standing up, Arbuckle nodded toward a narrow stairway leading toward a second story, said quietly, "Let's go," and, without looking at the girl, made for the stairs. She hesitated for just a moment, then, glacing at the bartender, shrugged her shoulders and followed.

"Each man had his needs," Augustino observed softly.

Sharp rose and walked outside, returning in a few minutes to sit back down and take another drink. Looking at Vent, he said, "No back stairway."

Vent nodded.

Borden chuckled. "The man who walks in on that

feller, no matter what he's doing, is going to damn sure regret it.''

Sharp watched the poker game for a few moments, then in an aside to The Preacher said, ''The slicker in the top hat is palming cards.''

The Preacher smiled. ''I noticed. Wanta take a hand?''

Sharp shrugged, glanced at Vent and, when Vent nodded, led the way to the table. ''Got room for a couple of fools who will probably be soon parted from their money?'' he asked.

The man in the top hat looked at Sharp and said softly, ''Owney Sharp.''

When The Preacher slid into a chair, the man next to him moved over to give him room, looking at him oddly. Probably trying to remember where he had heard of the ex-minister, Vent guessed, and he was right. The man suddenly exclaimed, ''Hell, you're The Preacher. I played cards with you in Odessa, Texas, once.''

The Preacher grinned frostily and said, ''You got a good memory, friend,'' and tossed a hundred dollars in gold to the dealer.

The game proceeded quietly for half an hour as Vent watched. Then, from upstairs, a cry penetrated the thin walls between the bar and the rooms, followed by several more cries, then silence. The players ignored them as did the rest of the patrons, although the bartender looked up the stairs nervously.

Sharp suddenly asked the man in the top hat, ''How old are you, friend?''

The gambler stared at Sharp, then said, ''I'm thirty-five, why?''

Sharp grinned, his hands lying quietly on top of his folded hand. ''Pretty young to cash in.''

"Huh?" the gambler said, and his face slowly turned white as he stared into Sharp's suddenly cold eyes.

"Palming cards isn't really the best way to guarantee longevity. I suggest you stop it, cash in and go find something less dangerous to do."

The Preacher seemed absorbed in his cards, but then he looked up and said softly, "Mr. Sharp, he's a real gentleman. Me, I've lived too long to be charitable. You just leave your chips where they lay and catch the next stage out. If I see you in town in the morning, I'll kill you."

Sharp glanced at The Preacher, then, looking back at the card cheat, observed, "Old Preacher, he sure is short-tempered. I reckon I'd do what he says . . . or stop by the undertaker and have him fit you out for a wooden overcoat 'cause if you don't leave town, you're gonna stay here permanently."

His face white, the gambler rose and quickly left the saloon. One of the men at the table observed, "That feller's one damn fool to try that kinda sandy with you gents playing. Wonder where he thought he was?"

"He was almost in hell," Sharp concluded, and the game went on, after the dealer raked the gambler's chips into the pot and announced the next winner would take all. Sharp won it.

Vent came over and said quietly, "I'll be down at the Clairborn getting us rooms. Me, I need a bath." Sharp and The Preacher nodded and went back to the game.

Arbuckle came downstairs, sat down and had another drink.

The bartender looked toward the stairs, but the girl did not appear.

Borden and Augustino rose and followed Vent toward the door.

"Where you fellers headed?" Arbuckle said.

"Clairborn," Vent said, and Arbuckle got up and went out with them.

When Vent walked in, the hotel clerk stared at him for a moment, then said, "Well, howdy Mr. Torrey. How the hell ya been?"

Vent smiled as he recalled the man and, shaking his hand, said, "Fine as Sunday on a spring morning. You got six rooms and about two hundred gallons of hot bathwater?"

"We can accommodate ya." The clerk spun the register as Vent listed their names and spun it back, then glanced down at them and whistled.

"We'll be riding out in the morning," Vent said, and turning, walked to the door, looked back and added, "Get that water ready. As soon as we take care of our horses, we'll be back."

As they led the animals along the street to the livery, Vent noted the marshal watching from his office window. When he finished putting up the Appaloosa, he left the others and walked to Crank's office and entered, took a chair and, placing his feet up on a dead stove, asked, "We got you some worried, Marshal?"

"Sorta," Crank admitted.

"Well, this here's the way it lays. Some fellers has took my sis and they got her hid out somewheres. They wanted me to do something I ain't inclined to do. I aim to get her back, but first I want to talk it over with Charlie. Those boys with me are just along for the ride."

Crank looked out the window as Vent's three companions entered the hotel. "Slab Borden, Angel Augustino,

Coup Arbuckle, The Preacher, Owney Sharp . . . pretty heavy company, I'd say.''

"They have a small piece of this," Vent admitted.

Crank looked at him and said quietly, "Me, I'm just a small-time town marshal. I ain't in any of you boys' class and never could be. If you wanted to, you could take this town apart and they'd be nothing I could do about it except get myself killed. I've heard good things about you, Mr. Torrey. I've heard you marshaled here and there and that you don't hunt trouble.''

"You heard right. I don't. Neither do the men I'm with. They ain't hellions. They've been around too long to act the damn fool. They's nothing in Crested Butte we want except a night's sleep, a hot bath, a little whiskey and a good meal or two.''

"Just so. You're welcome here, and if any of the citizens get a case of the braveries, I'd appreciate it if you'd let me handle it," Crank said.

"Agreed." Vent nodded, then told him, "Sharp and The Preacher are bucking the tiger over at the Sundance. Caught a feller in a top hat palming cards. Suggested he leave town or order up a pine box. He left. Hope that's all right.''

"You saved me the trouble. I was going to put him on the morning stage for Gunnison. I figured if he tried that down there, he'd get himself killed, but it wouldn't be in my town.''

Vent rose, shook hands and walked out.

Standing on the sidewalk looking toward the Clairborn, he had a sudden image of Lilly Tree, that wild lady drover he had fallen in love with when he first came to Colorado, running into the street to warn him the Hawkses were in town and laying for him.

Squinting his eyes, he marked the exact spot in the dust of the street where she fell, shot down by Hawkses' bullets. He had gone berserk then and in a savage, blazing gun battle had killed two of the Hawkses and left the front of the Clairborn riddled with bullet holes. He had almost died in that set-to until Charlie Brady took a hand. Brady was the town marshal in those days and a tough man to tangle with. Later, he had taken a bullet for Vent, lived to brag about it and eventually married Vent's sister Rhonda. Now Rhonda was in the hands of Stiles Burlingame-Leach and Vent had vowed he would get her back and at the same time make Leach and his fellow gamblers wish they had stuck to poker.

Charlie Brady was sitting on his front porch, rifle across his lap, when Vent and his fellow gunmen rode up through the lower field and stopped in front of the house. He looked at Vent for a long minute, then said, "Kind of an interesting bodyguard you got there, Vent."

Vent smiled. "Howdy, Charlie. Been awhile."

"I figured you'd be at Dead End."

"Nope. I brought Dead End along with me," Vent said.

Brady had his careful look at Vent's partners, then asked, "You planning on taking over Colorado?"

"No, just kicking up a little fuss with some fellers who got some kind of crazy idea they can kidnap a man's sister and force him to do their bidding. Figure to give them their needins."

"Light and come in," Brady invited. "I just put on a fresh pot."

Vent went inside and left the others to put up the horses. The hunchback turned the big stud loose in the field, not wanting him to kick Brady's corral to pieces.

"How come you put up with that mean varmint?" Borden growled.

"He suits me," Arbuckle replied. "How come you ride that ugly old mule?"

"He gets me where I want to go," Borden said, and bit off a huge chunk of tobacco. He hesitated for just a moment, looked at the hunchback, then offered him the tobacco and watched as he took a chunk out with strong white teeth.

Sharp, rubbing down his horse, said mildly, "That stuff'll corrode your guts, and when you get old, you'll go around with a bellyache all the time."

"Who the hell's going to live long enough to get old?" Arbuckle asked, watching his black stud roll in the grass.

"There's always that," Sharp said, and walked toward the house.

Augustino smiled, lit a cigar, blew smoke at the sky and wordlessly followed. Watching him walk away, Borden looked at Arbuckle and asked, "You ever see that feller break leather?"

"Yeah, once down in Tombstone. He shot three gents over a poker table so damn fast none of them got a gun out. He's hell on little red wheels."

"Can you beat him?" Borden asked curiously.

"Damned if I know," the hunchback said, and, turning his half-crazed eyes on the big man, added, "I'd sure as hell give her a whirl."

Brady looked at Vent and asked quietly, "How many men has that bunch out there accounted for?"

Vent thought it over for a moment, then said, "I reckon they've probably tallied about a hundred among the five of them, although The Preacher's never said much about his past.''

The door opened and the gunmen tramped inside. ''Pot's on, boys, help yourself,'' Brady said, then, turning to Vent, asked, ''You got any ideas about where Leach may have taken Rhonda?''

The Preacher turned and, steaming cup in hand, said, ''He owns a silver mine a day's ride west of Leadville toward Tennessee Pass. He's got her hidden up there in one of the mine shacks. The mine super's wife is guarding her.''

Vent stared at him, then looked back at Charlie and said, ''Well, I'll be damned.''

Arbuckle looked over the rim of his coffee cup and observed, ''That's one hell of a ride from here.''

''About three or four days,'' Sharp said.

''We'll leave in the morning,'' Vent decided. ''We can swing back through Crested Butte and pick up some grub and a pack horse and then cut through the Sawatch Range.''

The Preacher walked to the window and looked out, then said, ''Horseman coming.''

Brady rose and had his look, then turned to Vent and smiled. ''An old friend of yours.'' He stepped away from the window as Vent came and looked out. Coming along the trail from Lost Lake was an Indian riding a magnificent Appaloosa. The animal was all white with black spots over most of its body.

''Swift Wind,'' Vent said, and opened the door and stepped onto the porch. Raising his right hand, palm outward, he said, ''How, Swift Wind,'' and the Indian raised his hand and said, ''How, Leatherhand,'' and there was the old twinkle in his eyes as he looked down at the Missourian.

Swift Wind's hair was beginning to show white, yet he still sat his horse ramrod straight and he still carried himself like a true cavalry soldier of the Ute nation. It had been this Ute shaman who had devised Vent's leather hand for him after Vent saved Swift Wind's son from drowning in Lost Lake.

"Step down and come and sit with me," Vent invited.

Swift Wind nodded solemnly and dismounted lithely just as Vent's companions stepped onto the porch and stood in a line looking at him. He, in his turn looked back, made his silent inventory of each man and, looking at Vent said, "You travel with great warriors, old friend."

Turning, Vent said, "Boys, this here's Swift Wind, medicine man of the Ute nation. He's an old and valued friend." Pointing at each man Vent named them. The Indian repeated the names and Vent knew he would remember them as long as he lived.

They sat on the porch and Swift Wind looked into Vent's eyes and said, "You go on a great quest."

"Yep, I go looking for my sister. She was stolen by evil men."

"You will kill them?"

"More than likely." Vent nodded.

"She is a fine woman, as is her man, Charlie Brady. He has dealt fairly with me and my people and we have given him freedom to cross our lands and camp within their borders as long as he or his live here."

Charlie rose, walked to the porch and said, "Swift Wind, I know a friend when I'm faced with one. Now I need to call on that friend for help."

"Ask. Swift Wind is your friend," the Indian said solemnly.

"We plan to strike northeast to Leadville and beyond,"

Brady explained. "We need a guide through the Sawatch Range and north to the White River country."

"I know a way." Swift Wind nodded.

Vent asked, "You will guide us then?"

Swift Wind nodded. "I will guide you." He rose and went to his horse; mounting, he saluted the assembly and rode west toward the lake. Just as he reached the deeper timber he turned and called, "I'll return in the morning," and vanished.

"Now that there's one hell of an Injun," Borden observed.

"He's the most highly respected big medicine of all the tribes of the Ute," Brady said. "He can make predictions and they come true." Vent recalled the last time Swift Wind saw Lilly Tree. He had looked at her and said softly, "My friend, be kind to this woman. Her star is already at its peak and beginning to fall."

In less than a year, Lilly lay dead in the dust of a Crested Butte street, struck down by the Hawkses' bullets.

Vent crawled from his blankets at five the following morning and, walking quietly, moved outside to stand on the porch and keen the breaking light of dawn. Carefully he let his gaze traverse the lower pasture and the trail from Crested Butte, then turned and looked toward the saw-toothed peaks cutting off access to Lost Lake from the north.

These days he preferred sleeping outdoors and seldom availed himself of the accommodations of the towns he passed through. More and more he was becoming a solitary man who rode the high country alone, ever watchful, but glorying in the magnificent panoramas offered by the West. It was a place of high lonesome meadows, ragged cliffs, barren desserts, tall timber and wild lakes and rivers.

He loved every inch of it and no longer seemed happy unless he was riding the solitary ways.

"It's what makes this country worth staying in," Sharp, who had come quietly onto the porch, said from behind him.

Not looking around, Vent observed, "I fell in love with this here place when I first came from Kansas. It was here I wanted to stay for the rest of my life, but things happened and I had to move on."

"Brady said you lost a good woman here?"

"In Crested Butte. One of the Hawkses shot her. She was warning me of a trap." He looked up toward the meadow where Lilly Tree lay in eternal sleep and thought, I'll go up there in a few minutes and check the grave.

Then Brady thrust his head through the door, announced, "Breakfast will be up in about a half hour," and disappeared.

Vent and Sharp walked to the horse corral and checked on their mounts, then forked hay from a stack behind the small barn into the corral and, leaning on the top pole, watched them eat. A water trough just inside the corral needed refilling; taking a bucket from the fence, Sharp went to a spring up behind the barn and carried several bucketsful to the trough and filled it.

Arbuckle came along then, glanced at his stud, and the stud, sensing his master's examination, raised his head, laid his ears back and bared his teeth.

"Bastard," the hunchback snarled, and went and tossed some hay onto the grass for the big animal, who promptly tired to kick him and received a vicious whack on the flank from the pitchfork handle as Arbuckle dodged the flying hooves.

Shaking his head, Sharp observed, "That feller don't

have to worry about getting his ticket punched in a gunfight. Hell, that hoss'll kill him before that happens.''

The hunchback glanced at Sharp and grinned his flat, toothless grin, batted his half-crazed eyes and observed, ''Knew a gambler down in Sonora cut himself on the sharp edge of a playing card, got the poison and up and shoved in his chips in less than a week.''

Vent chuckled and headed for the house as Brady, head sticking out a window, called, ''Come and get it before I throw it out.''

The men sat around the long wooden table and forked meat from huge platters, piled biscuits beside the steaks, doused them liberally with meat gravy and fell to, downing cup after cup of powerful black coffee in the process.

As he sampled the coffee Augustino remarked, ''This would melt a concho, friend Brady, but that's the way I like it. Only you Americanos know how to make good coffee. In my country, it is always weak because people are poor and they cannot afford to put the proper amount of grind in.''

Looking at him curiously, Brady asked, ''You sound educated, Señor Augustino. Did you attend school in Mexico?''

''*Sí*. I went to the University of Mexico City for four years.''

Sharp raised his head and stared at him. He too had attended college, as had many men in the West in that era. The far western states were a conglomeration of men representing every walk of life. There were titled Englishmen, such as Stiles Burlingame-Leach, ignorant, poorly educated Irishmen from County Cork, Chinese mine workers, who brought to the West a thousand years of culture, and adventurers from half a dozen universities of the East, who had come seeking their fortune.

Vent knew many of them found only disappointment, and not a few, a lonely grave on boothill. Some, such as Owney Sharp, became deadly gunmen and lived until the edge of their speed began to wear away, then usually fell to a younger and faster gun. Thinking about this as he ate, he knew that someday, he, like others before him, would go down to a faster man if he stayed on the same trail he now rode. Then he told himself, you saddled this bronc, it's you that must ride him, and washed the bad thoughts from his mind. Half an hour later they were mounted and waiting for Swift Wind.

When he appeared, it was with all the fanfare an Indian is capable of generating. He was mounted on his spotted pony and wearing a traditional headdress that dangled down his back almost to his horse's withers. His powerful body was encased in beautifully worked white buckskin trimmed in dark beaver hide. He rode a cavalry saddle covered by a long, white buffalo robe, a mark of great prestige among Indians. Vent was surprised to see his Indian friend wearing a holstered .45 in a sagging shell belt around his narrow waist. A late model 38.40 Winchester rode in a buffalo-hide scabbard and on Swift Wind's left hip a huge bowie dangled freely in a rawhide sheath.

He came with five braves, all of them carrying late-model rifles and wearing handguns. Each rode a magnificent mount and each would have been a man to notice in any crowd.

Waving his hand to encompass his escort, Swift Wind said, "These men are the best fighters of my tribe. I and they are at your service, old friend."

Looking them over, Vent was glad they were on his

side. These were not ragtag leavings from the bottom of the tribal barrel. These were first-class fighting men who would count their share of coups in any battle.

Turning his horse, Vent gestured at the trail and, looking at Swift Wind, said, "It's your show, friend." He waited until the Indian trotted his horse forward, almost making a ceremony of it. As the animal passed Arbuckle's stud the brute reached a long nose out and attempted to take a bite from the spotted horse's hip. Swift Wind touched the animal with his heel and it slid gracefully away from the stud and moved out on the trail as the hunchback cursed and kicked the stud under the chin.

Chapter Five

She awoke to darkness, and, thinking for just a moment she was back home at Lost Lake, reached a hand for Charlie, then, when she felt only emptiness, realized with bitter sadness that he was not there and wouldn't be. Lying quite still, she stared at the blackness of the window on the far side of the room and was just able to make out the iron bars that kept her imprisoned here.

It was five A.M. and she was in bed in the bullion shack of the Grand Slam silver mine owned by Stiles Burlingame-Leach. She had been here for almost three weeks, held prisoner and watched over by Mrs. O'Rafferty, whose husband, Liam, was the superintendant of the Grand Slam.

Once, she had looked straight at the Irish woman and warned her, "My brother will come here soon and he'll kill your husband and anybody else who tries to stop him, and even though he is a gentleman, he may just hang you for kidnapping."

The woman laughed. "Your brother is off in Dead End

trying to stay alive. He won't come here. Missy, you best watch your tongue and mind your manners. You'll get along better.''

But she did not watch her tongue. Instead, she asked, ''Do you know who my brother is!''

The woman looked at her scornfully and said, ''Of course. He's a scalawag ne'er-do-well who rides around waving his pistol at honest folks and taking their money. Back home we had highwaymen like him and they soon found themselves swinging from the gibbet.''

She stared at the woman. It was no use, she decided. This woman had arrived from Ireland less than six months ago to marry Liam O'Rafferty. She could hardly know the rules of this new land. Maybe in Ireland they had no respect for women, but here in the West to kidnap a white woman and keep her imprisoned was a hanging offense, if the offender lived long enough to go to trial.

The bed was hard and the room stank. Several times since she had been imprisoned here, huge rats had run across her bed in the night, causing her to cry out in fright. Each time the woman had come to the door, looked in and ordered her to be quiet, then went away.

At first light there was the usual pounding on the door and orders in a broad Irish brogue to get up and start preparing the morning meal. Mrs. O'Rafferty had taken to forcing her to cook meals and clean the house, lording it over her as if she were a servant. Now she got up and, quickly disrobing, poured water from a pitcher into a large bowl and, shivering, gave her lush body a quick sponge bath. When she was finished, she dried off with the rough towel the woman had grudgingly provided her, dressed and went from the bullion shack along a narrow hall to the main house to begin breakfast.

When the meal was on the table, Mrs. O'Rafferty opened the door and called her man in from the porch where he had been sitting drinking his morning coffee. He came to the table, glanced at her and said, "Good morning, Mrs. Brady," and when Rhonda ignored him, fell to eating.

He was half through the meal when the front door suddenly opened and one of the mine workers, his face white, came in hurriedly and said, "Liam, you better come out here and quick," and turned and led the way outside. Rhonda went to a window and had her look. Then she said quietly, "You are about to meet that outlaw you've been making light of."

The Irishwoman came to the window and saw a tall young man wearing a black hat and heavy chaps sitting a magnificent horse. With him were five of the hardest-looking men she had ever seen and suddenly she was afraid. Afraid for her man and afraid for herself.

Rhonda calmly walked past her and stepped onto the porch. Vent looked at her, smiled, winked and, staring down at O'Rafferty, said quietly, "Mister, this just ain't yore day. I'm gonna hang you from the cross bar on that gate over there," and he pointed to a foot thick pole that lay across the top of two uprights flanking the entrance to the mine yard.

As he sat his horse, several men came from the mine, but when they saw the gunfighters, they stopped and hastily drew back, wanting no part of Vent's crew.

Mrs. O'Rafferty, who had followed Rhonda onto the porch, went to her man and, taking him by the arm, looked up at Vent and said sharply, "You murder my husband and I'll see you swing, Mr. Outlaw."

Owney Sharp chuckled. Doffing his flat black hat, he

said, "How long have you been over here from the old sod, ma'am?"

"I've been here all of six months," she said sharply, adding, "and what's it to you?"

"Well, it might just save you from a stretched neck," Arbuckle told her brutally.

Rhonda spoke up then from the porch. "She doesn't understand our ways yet, but she mistreated me and there's no excuse for that. Even in Ireland they must treat people properly."

Vent looked at her sternly. "Any excuses?"

"Since when must an honest Irishwoman make excuses to the likes of you?" the woman asked.

"Hang them both," Vent snapped, and rode to the porch, leaving a horrified Mrs. O'Rafferty standing in the dust of the yard.

Rounding on her then, her husband snapped, "Woman, when will you learn to keep yere face shut. You just don't know this country. These men mean business."

Slab Borden chuckled. "She'll keep her face closed once that rope shuts off her wind . . . permanently."

"Damn you," O'Rafferty shouted, and lunged for Borden, who calmly lifted a leg like a log and kicked the Irishman into the dust, where he lay stunned. Arbuckle dismounted and, jerking the man to his feet, led him to the gate, then turned to the woman. "Well, come along over here now. You can join yore old man in hell." Looking at The Preacher, he called, "Toss me a rope, Preacher, and dig out the Good Book. We should say a prayer for these fools."

One of the miners, more courageous than his fellows, stepped forward then, and, looking at Vent, said, "Don't you think hanging's just a little drastic?"

Vent looked at the ground for a moment, then glanced to where Arbuckle was fastening ropes around the O'Raffertys' necks and said, "They held my sister prisoner. The woman mistreated her. Mister, how long you lived out here?"

"Why, I been here a year," the miner replied.

"Then learn something from this and live to go back home someday," Vent told him. "Out here women are respected. A man who mistreats or otherwise harms a white woman can expect no mercy. A man who lays hands on a woman can expect a quick death and no one will stand up for him." Glancing at the O'Raffertys, he added, "If we were in the middle of Denver right now and the folks knew the story of what happened to my sister, they'd all want to pull on the rope. Why should I have mercy on these people?"

"Hell, for one thing, they're new to our ways," the man said, his voice bitter.

"There's such a thing as common decency no matter where a man comes from," Vent said, and there were cold winds in his voice.

Swift Wind, who had been sitting his horse near his braves at the edge of the yard, now rode forward and, nodding at O'Rafferty and his woman, asked, "Perhaps you should allow me to take these two. We need slaves at our camp."

The miner stared at the Indian, then pointed an accusing finger at Vent and said, "You'd sell these poor folks into slavery with the Injuns?"

"Better than hanging," Vent said bleakly. Riding to where the two stood with ropes around their necks, he looked down at O'Rafferty and asked, "What'll it be? A broken neck or a year working for Swift Wind?"

Mrs. O'Rafferty cried out, "No, Liam, they're savages. They'll do awful things to us. I heard all about 'em. They torture innocent folks."

Swift Wind tapped a heel against his horse and rode close to the woman. Leaning down, he stared at her, then letting his eyes wander over her ample frame, said softly, "You will be my seventh wife, after I work your husband to death," and he laughed evilly.

"Oh, my God in heaven," the woman cried out, and recoiled from the Indian, almost choking herself on the suddenly tightened rope.

O'Raffety was no fool. He was beginning to catch on to what was happening here. He also knew that the talk could go from joshing to death in a flash.

"I'll take my chances with the Injuns," he said, and Arbuckle looked at him and nodded. "Good choice, mister. Getting your neck stretched can be kinda permanent." He removed the rope from the frightened couple and nodded at Swift Wind. The Indian gestured at his braves; they came forward and led the O'Raffertys toward a corral where several horses were penned up.

Vent rode over, looked at the men and asked, "All of you here?"

The man who had gone to the O'Raffertys' defense nodded and said. "Yes, sir. This is all of us. You fixing to hang us too."

"You have anything to do with keeping my sister here?" Vent asked.

"Hell no," the man said. "We warned O'Rafferty he could get in trouble out here for that kinda trick. He wouldn't listen. Seems Mr. Leach told him you fellers was killers and outlaws."

"You know me?" Vent asked.

The man shook his head. An oldster who had been quietly watching the proceedings now came forward and said, "I know you, Leatherhand. I know your friends too." He looked at the first miner and, nodding at Vent, told him, "This here feller has worked as a city marshal in several towns in Colorado."

"He has?"

"Yep, and O'Rafferty's damn lucky to be alive. In this country treating a woman as he treated Mrs. Brady is more than enough to get a man hanged. Someday, after he's been out here awhile, he'll realize Mr. Leatherhand let him off damn easy, sending him and his missus along with the Injuns."

Looking at Vent, the miner asked, "What you gonna do with us?"

"Nothing," Vent said, adding, "but you'd best ride on. Before we leave here there'll be no mine or anything else. He lifted his chin to where Slab Borden, an expert at blowing safes, was busily planting dynamite around the buildings, removing sticks from several cases he had brought from the powder shed.

A third miner came forward and looked nervously at Borden. "If that feller don't know what he's doing, he could blow us all up with that stuff."

"Who are you?" Vent asked.

"I'm the powder monkey." The miner still watched Borden, who was going about his work with a scowl on his face while humming softly to himself.

"He knows what he's doing," Vent assured the miner, then pointing toward the corral, ordered, "You boys pick up your possibles, catch a horse and ride to hell outa here."

After the men had gone, Vent rode to where Swift Wind

waited and, lifting his hand, said, ''How,'' and the Indian, a twinkle in his eye, returned the salute and led his men into the timber. As they passed from view, O'Rafferty tossed one last forlorn look over his shoulder and Vent thought, you're lucky, friend, lucky I don't like hanging, and went to search the super's house to see if there was anything there he could use against Leach.

Borden, his work done, rode to the porch of O'Rafferty's house and called, ''Vent, she's ready.''

They waited on a ridge half a mile to the south while Borden fired his charges, then mounted the mule and rode leisurely toward them. He was a hundred yards from the ridge top when the first charge blew. He did not look back. The mule merely flicked one long ear as the second and third charges went up.

It was a spectacular sight. The buildings seemed to come apart as the charges exploded under them. Timbers were hurled through the air and pieces of tin from the roofs sailed away like giant metallic leaves, landing with a clatter amid the boulders tossed from a monster tailing pile.

When the blast went off above the mine, Vent knew Leach would have to dig mighty deep in his wallet to come up with the kind of money it was going to require to remove the overburden that now came cascading down the mountain to bury the mine entrance in tons of rock and dirt. A pillar of dust spiraled skyward for three hundred feet and rocks and large boulders rained down among the exploding buildings.

Sharp drew in his breath and said, ''That's the way hell's gonna be,'' and Arbuckle grinned at him from his half-crazed eyes and replied, ''They ain't no doubt you'll have a chance to find out.''

Vent said, "Let's ride," and led the way down into the timber where Charlie Brady waited anxiously by a big pine tree. When Rhonda saw him, she jumped down, ran straight into his arms and hugged him. Then she looked up into his face and said, "Oh Lord, Charlie Brady, how I've missed you."

"I'd have come for you long before this, but I knew that you'd want Vent to have a chance," he said huskily, and Vent looked away as the distant rumble of the exploding mine sent its echoes cascading down the mountains. He had deliberately left Brady behind in case there was gun trouble. He did not want to have to worry about a man making a mistake because his wife was in the thick of things. Brady had argued but in the end had seen the wisdom in the thing and so had waited. Now he had his beautiful Rhonda back and that was all that mattered.

They mounted, and, holding hands, followed the gun-men down the mountain.

Vent rode into Denver just as the sun rose above the flat prairie land that stretched almost unbroken from the Rocky Mountains to Independence, the jumping-off place for wagon trains on their way west to California, Oregon and points in between.

The city of Denver, for city it was by the beginning of the eighties, boasted 30,000 souls, and was a turbulent, busy community where merchants were becoming rich outfitting miners and furnishing mining equipment for the hundreds of silver strikes around Leadville, Central City, Blackhawk, Dogtown, Mountain City and Nevadaville.

These mines were producing millions and it all came to Denver, pouring over the bars in torrents and being spent on new buildings, art centers and grand theaters.

Denver was the trade center of the Rocky Mountains, but Vent had no interest in silver or silver mines other than those owned and operated by five wealthy men.

As he rounded into Larimer Street, with its dozens of establishments catering to the needs of mines and miners, he noted a small sign halfway along the block that extended a short distance out over the wooden sidewalk proclaiming the headquarters of Burlingame-Leach Enterprises. As Vent neared the office, a man stepped through the front door and onto the sidewalk, half turned and, upon seeing Vent, stopped and became suddenly still and watchful.

As he rode toward him, Vent had his look and knew this was the man described by Rhonda as having kidnapped her. He wore two guns in low-cut holsters tied to his thighs. Their butts canted slightly forward within easy reach of his seemingly casual hands, but Vent knew better than to think the gunman had not recognized him or was not ready to go into instant action.

Stopping the Appaloosa twenty feet from where the man stood, Vent nodded casually, rolled a cigarette, then gazed solemnly at the gunman through a haze of blue tobacco smoke.

"Nice day," he said.

"Reckon," the man answered, and leaned a shoulder—his left one—against a porch support.

Vent smiled bleakly but there was no merriment in his eyes. They looked a thousand years old as he stared down at the stranger.

"Help ya?" the man asked.

"Maybe," Vent countered, and dropped his right hand over the saddle horn.

The gunman's eyes flicked to the leather-covered hand and then up to Vent's face and Vent saw a look of bleak acceptance in the man's eyes as he straightened up from the porch support and spread his feet slightly.

"You can't beat me, you know," Vent said softly, and was aware of the sidewalks suddenly emptying as shoppers ducked into stores, expecting gunfire at any moment.

"I'm paid to try," the man said.

"What's a life worth?" Vent asked curiously. He really wanted to know.

The gunman looked puzzled for a moment, then shrugged. "Whatever price the owner puts on it," he said.

Vent smiled. "Good answer," and drew and fired and watched his bullet take the gunman just over the heart and slam him back against the face of the building. He hung there for a second, his mouth stretched wide in agony, then slid to a sitting position with his feet before him and his head on his chest. In that position, he quietly died.

A tall man wearing a badge came along the street, leaned over and peered into the dead man's face, then straightened up and looked at Vent. "Deadern' a nit," he said.

"I reckon," Vent agreed.

"You got a reason for this?" the lawman asked.

"He helped some fellers kidnap my sister." Vent nodded and rode back along the street where curious onlookers stared at him as he passed.

Five miles south of Denver on the Colorado Springs trail, Vent turned off into a grove of oak trees and rode into a narrow hollow where the others lay around a small campfire sleeping, playing cards or drinking coffee.

Dismounting, Vent off-saddled and staked the Appaloosa in a small green meadow to the west. A sweetwater spring drained on the grass, affording natural irrigation. As the Appy bent its head and began feeding, Arbuckle's stud sidled up and reached out to take a tentative nip from his shoulder.

Looking up, the hunchback shouted, "Get away from there, you mangy bastard." He leaped to his feet, picked up a large rock and hurled it at the animal. The stud snorted and dodged the rock expertly, looked at his master with bared teeth, then ambled off, nipping at the grass.

Borden, playing two-handed solitaire with the Mexican, looked up, and scowled. "If that brute belonged to me, I'd pop a blue whistler through its skull."

"A man who rides a mule ain't got much to brag about," Arbuckle retorted.

Vent filled a cup with hot black coffee, sipped it, made a face and came over to squat beside Sharp. "Scratch one," he said.

Hearing him, the other men turned and waited. "Caught Williams in front of Leach's office on Larimer Street. He was pretty slow."

The Preacher, who had been stretched out on his back asleep, raised up on an elbow and asked Vent. "Now what?"

"Now we hit Deak Hammer where it hurts the most," Vent replied.

"We gonna rob his bank?" Slab asked eagerly.

"Nope, we're gonna do more than that. We're gonna cause a run on it."

"A run, señor?" Augustino said, and began to smile.

"That's right. A run. We'll drift into town one at a time, circulate around the saloons and start talk about how Deak Hammer's left the country because his bank and other holdings are in financial trouble. Then I'll stage a little one-act play at the bank."

Sharp shook his head in admiration. "You know, Mr.

Leatherhand, you never cease to amaze me. For a feller who was raised down in the Missouri breaks, you sure do come up with some slick plans. How come you know about bank runs?''

Vent grinned. "Saw one once down at Creede. Folks went crazy. Lined up clean through town and threatened to lynch the banker if he didn't give 'em their money. Had to call out the army to get it stopped.''

"Was it a real shortage?'' Sharp asked.

"Yep, that one was. The banker had stolen most of the folks' money.''

"What happened to him?'' Arbuckle said.

"They finally hanged him,'' Vent said.

The Preacher sat up and leaned his elbows on his knees. "Vent's right. I witnessed a couple of them things myself. Folks go crazy when they think they're gonna lose their money. And it'd be real easy to start a run just the way Vent laid her out.''

"What you plan on doing in the bank?'' Borden asked.

"Watch,'' Vent advised, and went and sat on his saddle blanket. Unholstering his .44, he began carefully stripping it down, using a small penknife to remove the necessary screws. Digging cleaning material from his saddlebags, he methodically removed powder accumulations from the moving parts and dressed them with a thin film of oil, then swabbed out the barrel and put the weapon back together. Using a dry cloth, he carefully removed all excess oil from the metal parts and made sure none clung to the grips or outside of the trigger assembly. He had heard of at least one man who died because his hand slipped on oil missed when he cleaned his weapon shortly before a fight.

Watching him, Borden asked, "You think that there .44 is a better chunk of iron than the Colt .45?''

"I reckon it's what you get used to, Slab. Me, I been totin' this here .44 around since I was a boy. Paw bought it for me and taught me how to shoot it when I was nine. It's an old friend."

Borden reached to his saddle and slapped the sawed-off shotgun that hung in its special holster from the saddle horn. "This here's my salivator. When I cut down with that old double bore, a man don't get a second chance."

Arbuckle grinned. "The trick, of course, is to get it into action before the other gent plugs you fulla holes."

Scowling, Borden observed, "I figure I can take at least four slugs before I go down. During the time it takes a man to reach me with them, I'll get off both barrels of that old Greener. I may cash in, but so will he. How many fellers you know want to chance them kinda odds?"

Vent stood up and, looking down at Borden, smiled. "I ain't one of 'em." He walked over to the spring and had his drink, then came back, carried his blanket and saddle across the clearing and dropped them beside a large boulder, smoothed out the blanket and lay down. He was asleep almost immediately.

He left a puzzled Slab Borden, who wasn't used to a gunfighter who admitted he might not want to fight for fear of the odds.

It was two P.M. in the afternoon and all morning a crowd had been gathering in the street before the Bank of Denver. As bank clerks peered anxiously from front windows, the muttering increased, then a tall man in a grey hat entered the building and walked to one of the clerk's cages, where he proffered a hundred-dollar bill and asked that it be cashed. The obliging clerk complied and the tall man folded the money and walked outside, then stopped and carefully counted it. When one of the bystanders noticed him, the tall man said, "I reckon I'm lucky to get my money, the shape that there bank's in." Several well-dressed men gathered around the stranger and began asking questions so fast he finally held up his hand and said, "Hey, now boys, one at a time."

A rail-thin oldster wearing a bowler hat and mourning coat crowded forward and demanded, "Is it true, young feller? Is this bank going under?"

The tall man said quietly, "My uncle owns some stock in her and he told me last night old Deak's in deep trouble. Poor old boy's about broke. Reckon he'll have to close her down soon. Feller'd be lucky to wind up with five cents on the dollar. . . ."

Meanwhile, five hard-looking men drifted from saloon to saloon and hotel to hotel. At each place they started a conversation; it led to the condition of Deak Hammer's bank. It was going under. Anyone who had money there was bound to lose it. Hammer was overextended. He had invested his money recklessly and carelessly.

One of the men spreading the story, a tall old man who carried a Bible and sat quietly reading it in hotel lobbies, was very convincing. Those who met him told others about the Bible thumper who knew Deak Hammer personally and was praying for him, but that it was probably too late altready, that he would soon be stony broke.

The run began at ten A.M. the next day and by noon the bank was cleaned out of ready cash and the manager was desperately trying to borrow enough from one or another of his competitors to bail it out. When no other banker would take the chance without Deak Hammer's personal assurances, the manager closed the doors and quietly slipped out the back, to the stable, where he saddled a fast horse, rode hard to the west, finally stopping in San Francisco. There he took a job on the docks, unloading ships.

The clerks, taking their cue from the manager, also left town hurriedly, leaving the bank closed, locked and empty of funds.

As the Denver business community boiled with speculation, Vent led his men out of town and rode for Fort Morgan and the 70,000-acre ranch owned by Amos Dewberry.

They hit Dewberry's herds three days later, driving 1,500 head northeast toward the Kansas line, keeping ten miles south of the Platte River. Two days' drive along the Platte and Vent swung the lead steer due east toward Frenchman's Creek; five days later, he pushed the stock onto a bedground five miles south of Venango, a huddled group of squatty adobes located on the Kanasas-Colorado line and frequented by outlaws, gamblers, horsethieves and rustlers.

Arbuckle and Augustino took the first watch, slowly riding around the weary herd while the rest of the men made camp in a shallow depression on a small hill. Fifty feet below lay the flat stretch of barren country where the cattle either rested or wandered about feeding on the buffalo grass.

Sitting over a cup of coffee and a plate of beans and tortillas, Vent slowly spooned the food into his mouth and chased it down with frequent gulps of the hot brew. He was gut tired and ready for his bedroll but knew he must forgo such luxury until he and Borden made contact with the big gunman's cow buyer, who was to meet them in Venango at Carter's Midnight Palace, a sprawling saloon and general store run by a former sutler retired from the Union Army.

Finishing his coffee and beans, Vent rose and dropped the soiled utensils on a square of canvas Borden, who had turned out to be a pretty fair camp cook, had placed on the ground for that purpose. Looking at the big man, Vent said, "You about ready to ride, Slab?"

Wordlessly, Borden removed the dirty cloth he had worn tucked into his belt for an apron, lifted his shotgun rig from the horn of his saddle and buckled it around his waist, picked up the saddle and went for his mule.

"Reckon you better come along too, Owney," Vent said, and Sharp gathered up his gear and followed along to where the horses were staked out.

An hour later, they rode into Venango's main street and pulled up to study the town. Vent had his look and wasn't impressed. The sun beat down on the dusty street where half a dozen horses tied to hitching posts in front of Carter's Midnight Palace stood hipshot and swished flies. A dog lay in the dirt just off the sagging wooden sidewalk fronting a gun repair shop. A man wearing an apron and a dirty, crumpled hat swept dirt from the doorway of a small building halfway along the street. Over the door a sign proclaimed this was the Paradise Café. The remainder of the adobes apparently housed the handful of citizens who called Venango home.

"Hell-of-a-lookin' layout, ain't she?" Borden said.

"Not much of an excuse for a town," Sharp agreed.

Vent did not like the feel of the place and was about to say so when six riders walked their horses from a narrow alley into the middle of the street, turned them toward Vent and his companions and pulled them to a stop thirty feet away.

One of the riders, a broad-shouldered man sporting a sweeping mustache and hair that hung to his shoulders, reached up with his left hand and pushed his wide-brimmed hat to the back of his head and smiled. The smile didn't quite reach his eyes. "Seems to me you boys sorta got mixed up back at Fort Morgan and kinda left with a herd of cows that belonged to another man," he said.

Vent nodded his head gravely. "You're right in most respects, friend, but wrong in one important one. . . ."

"Oh?" and the long-haired rider glanced around at his friends, shrugged, looked back at Vent and waited stolidly.

"Yep, we left with cows that didn't belong to us, but we weren't mixed up. We took them deliberately and what's more, neighbor, we aim to keep them, at least until a buyer shows interest."

"The hell ya say?" the rider exclaimed.

A bony-faced man with a wicked scar reaching from eyebrow to chin pushed his horse in front of the long-haired man's mount and said, "You heard this feller, Jesse. He just admitted he's a damn cow thief."

"I sure as hell did," Vent assured him.

"Well, I'll be damned," a thin reed of a man, wearing two guns and riding a hammer-headed grulla, growled. "Admitted it plain as the nose on yore face."

Sharp suddenly chuckled, his voice a whiplash, then snapped, "You, in the back there! Keep your hand away from that gun unless you want to quit punching cows and go to wrangling clouds."

There was a quick stirring among the horses as five of the riders moved away from the culprit and left him facing Vent and his friends alone.

The man called Jesse looked at Sharp for a long time then asked, "Don't I know you from somewhere?"

"Coule be. I been somewhere," Sharp said laconically.

The skinny rider suddenly snapped, "To hell with all

this palaver, Jesse. Let's us just hang 'em. They done said they did it."

Vent watched the long-haired man, noted the indecision on his face, then asked quietly, "You Dewberry's ramrod?"

"Name's Jesse Strather and I'm Dewberry's ramrod."

"Well, Mr. Strather, you're into something you know nothing of," Vent said, then nodded toward the thin rider and warned, "You listen to that waddy and he'll get you pushed between a rock and a hard place."

"I know a cow thief when I see one," the skinny rider said, and he urged his horse out in front of the others and dropped his hand to his gun butt.

"You either pull that gun or take your hand to hell away from it," Vent warned, and there was something in his voice that froze the thin rider.

Borden, who had been silently watching the byplay, now rode his mule out to the left and pulled him in. The foreman looked at him sharply, then his eyes turned dead cautious as he took in the deadly-looking shotgun and the black mule. "Slab Borden," he said softly.

An older rider who had been sitting his horse just behind Strather now rode around him and had his look. Turning his horse sharply, he rode toward the alley without looking back.

Strather stared after him, then half turning his mount, called, "Hey, Andy . . . Where the hell you going?"

"West," the rider said, and did not slow his pace.

Looking back at Vent, Strather asked, "Who the hell are you men?"

Sharp smiled and nodded at Vent. "This feller's called Leatherhand. Me, I'm Owney Sharp."

Slab peeled back his lips in a humorless smile and said, "In case you split up your bunch and sent half of them out to bring back the herd, I'll tell who they're gonna meet up with out there. They's Coup Arbuckle, Angel Augustino and The Preacher.''

Strather stared. ''What the hell's six gunfighters doing stealing cattle?'' he asked in wonder.

''We love the taste of beef,'' Sharp said, and grinned.

Vent was in no mood to waste more time. He decided to push this man and see what happened. ''You got a choice, Mr. Ramrod. Pull iron or take your men and ride out. If you did send somebody out to the herd, you best stop by boothill and dig a few holes for them.''

''We didn't figure we'd need more men,'' Strather said sullenly. ''Hell, we never figured we'd have to buck the six fastest guns around.''

''I told you you know nothing of what's involved here,'' Vent said. ''We got no quarrel with you or your men. We don't want to bust caps on you, but on the other hand, you get a case of the braveries and you're gonna wind up history.''

Glancing around at his men, Strather said, ''Come on boys. We ain't getting paid fighting wages and we damn sure ain't getting paid to match guns with fellers like these. Let's ride.''

Watching them, Vent suddenly knew the slim rider was one of those men who couldn't back down, couldn't leave it alone. He was going to show fight; for just a moment the Missourian felt a deep reget, then thought, let it be on his head.

He was right. The rider, his face set in a hard frown, said harshly, ''You may back water to these gunnies, but they don't scare me one damn bit. I come after cows and by God I'm gonna get 'em if I have to gun somebody.''

Borden shook his head, said softly, ''Damn foool,'' and

suddenly the shotgun was in his fists and flame and smoke belched from the left-hand bore. As the startled Dewberry riders fought to control their horses, the skinny rider took the charge full in the chest and was driven backward over his horse's withers to slam into the dust of the street, dead when he hit the ground.

"Damn!" Strather said bitterly.

Sharp, his hand on his gun butt, said, "Pick up your dead and ride out, Mr. Strather. . . . Now!"

Nodding at two of his riders, the foreman sat his still-restless horse and watched dispassionately as they dismounted, heaved the blood-drenched body across the saddle and lashed it there with the dead man's own rope while his mount kept stepping sideways and snorting.

Handing the rope to one of the others, the two men stepped into saddles and Strather sat and looked at Vent for a long time, then said, "I've heard you were a fair man, Leatherhand. I surely do hope you got one hell of a good reason for this day's work."

"I have," Vent said, then making a decision, told him, "You tell Dewberry that kidnapping my sister is going to be the last mistake he ever makes." Leaving the startled foreman staring, he turned his horse and rode to a hitch rack in front of the Midnight Palace, stepped down and tied up.

Strather led his men out of town, their passing marked by a trail of blood leaking from the chest-torn victim of Borden's shotgun.

Half a dozen men standing on the sidewalk in front of the saloon made way for Vent and his companions as they pushed through the batwings and walked to a table near the back of the room.

Sharp detoured to the bar and ordered a bottle and glasses and then joined Vent and Borden.

"Ever notice how a feller will talk his way right out of livin'?" Sharp asked.

"They's a hell of a lot more damn fools in this world than smart men," Vent said.

The bartender brought over the bottle and glasses and was followed by a heavy-set man sporting a walrus mustache and wearing a flat-crowned Texas Stetson.

"Howdy, Slab," he said, and Borden nodded, tipped his chin at the table and said, "Jack Krause, this here's Owney Sharp and Vent Torrey, the feller they call Leatherhand."

Krause nodded at each in turn and Vent, looking him over, decided he was probably an old-time rancher who had turned to cattle buying when the winters got too long and the summers too hot.

"We got 1,500 head of prime beef south of town," Borden said. "What's beef bringing now?"

Krause knew better than to try and run a sandy on Borden, and Vent could see it in the man's eyes. He was afraid, yet his pride would not allow him to show it. Now he glanced at a chair, said, "I'm gettin' kinda old and broken down. Mind if I sit?"

Vent pushed the chair out with a boot toe and watched Krause slide into it. "Prime's bringing twelve on the hoof," he said.

Borden glanced at Vent and asked, "That satisfy you?"

Vent nodded and Borden turned back. "Sold," he said. Looking up to where the bartender stood leaning against the backbar, he motioned for another glass by holding up his own, and one finger. When the glass was delivered, he poured Krause a drink and lifted his glass in salute. "To a deal," he said, and drank it off.

"Like to ask you a question," Krause said, placing his empty square in front of him.

"Fire and fall back," Borden invited.

"Was that little set-to out there in the street related in any way to these cattle?"

Vent could see the man didn't like having to ask it, but he also knew that if Krause ignored it, he was a damn fool and he didn't appear to be stupid.

Borden grinned. "Yep, them boys ride for Amos Dewberry. We stole them cows from Dewberry's Wagon Tongue-T outfit at Fort Morgan and they sorta wanted them back."

"Then I reckon I'd best round up some riders and push them further east," Krause said offhandedly.

"Might not be a bad idea," Sharp agreed, and rose as Vent pushed back his chair and led the way outside. Stepping through the batwings he had his quick look along the street to the north, knowing either Borden or Sharp would check to the south.

Krause excused himself and walked down street, knocking on several doors as he went. Each time he paused at one of the adobes, a man would come out, look toward Vent and his friends, nod and reenter the houses, then reappear, strapping on gun belts and carrying rifles encased in leather scabbards. By the time the cattle buyer had reached the livery stable, he had eight men following him. Five minutes later they came out of the barn riding tough desert horses and followed by a man driving a chuck wagon.

Vent led them south and that afternoon was spent making the tally. Once Krause was satisfied with the count, he rode over to Borden and stepped down. The big gunman and the buyer squatted in the grass and finished their business. Krause counted out eighteen thousand dollars in gold neat stacks on the ground and, when Borden said he was satisfied, replaced the money in a leather sack and handed it over.

They did not shake hands and Borden did not give Krause a bill of sale. He didn't have to. Krause had one already jerry-rigged a week earlier.

Nodding at him, Borden said, "Nice doing business with you, as usual." Gathering up the sack, he rode to where Vent waited. Tossing the sack to the Missourian, the big gunman grinned and said, "Operating capital. I'll get mine later."

Vent nodded and wordlessly dropped the sack in the saddlebag, then led the gunmen west, keeping well to the south of the Platte River and on the second day cutting southwest toward the Big Sandy.

They rode into the small settlement of Rocky Ford four days later and stopped long enough to eat, wash the dust from their throats with half a dozen shots of raw whiskey chased by warm beer. Sharp purchased a new supply of cigars and Borden led their pack horse across the street to the mercantile and bought grub and a half dozen large canvas water bags and extra metal canteens for each man. Half an hour later, he returned to the saloon and announced the canteens and bags were full of fresh water and the pack horse loaded and ready to move.

Nodding at the bartender, Vent dropped a coin on the plank and led his companions through the batwings into the street. Two hours later they were riding the old Timpas trail toward Tyrone on the La Junta-to-Trinidad road.

Each man now carried his Winchester across the pommel of his saddle. This was Comanche country and a man who didn't ride with eyes in the back of his head and ears stretched out a foot didn't live long, Vent knew.

Once they crossed the tracks of several unshod horses and Vent stopped the Appaloosa for a closer examination. Looking up at Sharp, he said, "Eight riders. Traveling fast to the west. Probably a hunting party."

"Or a scalping party," Arbuckle said, and grinned and batted his half-crazed eyes.

Vent stared at him and suddenly realized the hunchback would like nothing better than tangling with a war party. And with that realization came a complete understanding of Coup Arbuckle. He was a man who loved to fight and the devil take the odds. If he went down, then fate had the hand, and if he won, the devil was riding his cantleboard. Vent had met one or two like him along his backtrail, and although he recognized them for what they were, he did not understand them.

Men called the Coup Arbuckles of the world "the untoward" and Vent knew that meant they cared for nothing on the face of the land. They did what pleased them, and if there were objections, then so much the better. And always someone died. Always someone went down under the gun when the untoward became restless. Knowing this, Vent also knew the hunchback would play this game until he became bored then he would either ride out with a casual wave of the hand or challenge one of them and go for the gun.

When that happens, he thought, I'll have to kill him, and he remounted and moved on south. It was a long three-day ride from Rocky Ford to Trinidad. They rode into the Mexican pueblo at midnight.

As they walked their horses along the dusty street, loud

shouts came from the open doors of cantinas; the shapeless shadows of men on the move from one saloon to another would suddenly take on human form as they passed lighted windows, then become will-o'-the wisps again as they moved on.

A fight suddenly erupted just inside the open door of a cantina they were passing and two men locked in combat burst from the place, staggered across the sidewalk and fell almost beneath Augustino's horse's hooves, wringing a curse from the Mexican as his horse sidestepped to avoid the heaving bodies.

"*Cabrons*," Augustino snarled, but the smile stayed in place.

Arbuckle suddenly pulled his horse into a dusty, rutted side street leading to the gaping doors of a livery stable half a block off Main and the others followed him. Drawing up before the place, he sat contemplating the dark maw of the barn until a heavy-set man came out, pulling his suspenders over powerful shoulders. The hunchback looked at him and said, "Need livery for six horses. Bait of grain, good hay . . . no dusty stuff . . . rubdowns all the way around and careful watering."

Looking over his potential customers, the livery stable owner decided he would do exactly what he had been told to do by the man with the crazy eyes. Vent could read the decision on his face as he pushed the Appy forward; stepping down, he said, "Watch the black my friend here's topping. He's mean as hell. Kick the hat off yore head you get within gunshot distance of him. Best turn him out in the corral and leave the gate open. He'll stay. You can stall the rest."

Arbuckle grinned as he dismounted and led the stud inside while the owner cautiously moved out of the way, watching the animal's swinging head and wild eyes as it bared its teeth and snapped at the air.

"Sonofabitch," the hunchback snarled, and wrapped the loose ends of his reins around the brute's neck twice. Instead of backing off, the big black charged Arbuckle, who neatly sidestepped, then flipped the long reins around its forefeet and jerked it to its knees.

"You fall on my saddle, you ornery varmint, and I'll put a blue whistler through yore head," Arbuckle snarled as the stud, not in the least chastised, struggled to its feet.

The livery man turned to Vent and asked in wonder, "Why would a man ride that kind of horse?"

Vent grinned. "You'd have to ask him, but if I was you, I'd be kinda careful just how you put it to him. He's about as mean as that damn stud."

The owner kept his peace and Vent led the gunfighters from the stable back to the main street. As they moved south along the wooden sidewalk, men took one look and stepped hurriedly into the street to let them pass. A drunk who staggered from a cantina and bumped into Borden was promptly heaved into the street, where he landed with a loud grunt amid a cloud of dust. They moved on.

Vent turned in at a café and the gunmen tramped down the almost block-long room and took a large table in the shadows near the back. Ordering beans and frijoles, sided by fried potatoes and a slab of steak, they fell to.

Vent finished his meal, rolled a cigarette and lit it and then leaned back and watched Borden put away his third steak. The owner came back and stared at the big man's plate, then asked, "You got a holler leg, or something?"

Borden turned his massive head and leveled a cool look at the man. "Bring another, and make it a decent cut this time."

Sharp, cigar in the corner of his mouth, coffee cup in hand, smiled, and then suddenly set the cup gently on the table, nodding toward the kitchen. ''You had best go back to your stove, feller.'' The man, sensing something in the gambler's voice, glanced around and then hurried toward his kitchen just as the back door slammed wide on its hinges and a rifle barrel appeared in the entrance.

Vent drew and fired three rapid shots into the black opening and was rewarded by someone's death scream, then men seemed to appear from everywhere.

Two chap-clad figures vaulted the counter, guns in hand, and were cut down by the double explosions of Borden's murderous shotgun. They hit the floor screaming as the front door burst inward and men crowded the entrance, firing as they came.

''Oh my God,'' the proprietor screamed as he dropped with four stray slugs in his body.

The Preacher was leaning forward, slip-hammering his deadly Colts as Augustino crouched over his twin .45s, their barrels spouting tunnels of flame, while Coup Arbuckle, laughing insanely, poured lead into a tall man with a high-crowned hat who crouched over his blazing gun near the end of the counter. The tall man took the hunchback's slug square through the breastbone and was slammed back and down, leaving a smear of blood on the wall behind him to mark his passing.

Borden, roaring, sprang onto the table, drew his huge bowie knife and leaped onto these men who were trying to rush them. As he slashed wildly in all directions, the blade severed one man's arm. The unfortunate victim stared in horror as the member skittered across the tabletop and dropped from view beneath The Preacher's feet. A second victim died with Borden's blade buried hilt deep in his neck, and the third man, suddenly terrified of this huge, bloody apparition, broke and ran for the door only to be cut down by Sharp, who planted a slug in the center of the man's back.

"Back door!" Vent shouted, and hammered three shots into the bodies of two gunmen who had dived through the opening headfirst and landed rolling along the floor in an attempt to avoid the gunfighter's sizzling lead. Vent pounded his slugs into them and they lay still. Crouched over his smoking six, he punched out the empties and quickly reloaded just as Sharp gave forth a wild Rebel yell and charged around the table, blasting away the last four slugs in his guns.

Vent, trying to identify friend from foe, peered through the billowing black powder smoke that now filled the room and was afraid to fire for fear he would hit one of their own. Then the hunchback came out of the gloom and, eyes wild with blood lust, shouted, "They hit the street!" then broke for the door with Vent and The Preacher close behind.

As they burst through the opening onto the sidewalk, gun flame streaked out from an alley near a cantina and both Vent and The Preacher answered in kind. As their twin slugs whipped into the alley, a man screamed and collapsed into the dust, the light from the cantina bathing his bloody face in dark lines.

Someone down the street fired and was answered by the booming detonation of Borden's shotgun. Vent figured the big man had left by the back door, circled around and come up an alley down street. His shot sent a cupful of buckshot into a man's body; Vent watched as the corpse was hurled completely over a water trough and sent tail over boots into the middle of the main drag.

Now bullets began peppering the walls of the café from

a narrow notch between two buildings half a block north and Vent ran crouching along the front of the business establishments on the east side of Main, shooting from the hip as he ran. As he passed an open doorway, someone fired almost point-blank at him and miraculously missed. Vent twisted away, turned in midstride to hammer a bullet into a dark shadow lurking there. He was rewarded by a sudden grunt, a hacking cough and then a stocky man, mouth stretched wide in a dying grimace, measured his length on the wooden walk.

Somewhere Angel Augustino laughed wildly and Vent heard his twin .45s begin to sing a death knell. Running north, he broke across the street directly into someone's fire and felt the hot branding-iron touch of a bullet along his rib cage. Then he was firing back; someone screamed and died in a dark alley and Vent crossed the street, crouched in a doorway to reload, then broke back south. As he passed the open doorway of a cantina, he glanced inside and saw the place was empty. A bullet smashed the window just behind him and he ran on.

Sharp suddenly appeared out of the gloom and said sharply, "Vent?"

"Here," Vent answered, and the two met near a narrow notch between buildings. The Missourian stood by while the gambler reloaded, then asked, "Know where the others are?"

Sharp nodded toward the east side of the street and said, "Over there somewhere. Who the hell are these people?"

"Don't know," Vent answered, "but they sure as hell don't like us," and he fired at a shadow as someone ran along the boardwalk, his bootheels pounding at the wood as he tried to get clear in a driving run that suddenly deteriorated into a headlong collapse into a water trough.

"Vent?" Borden called from near the restaurant.

"Here" Vent answered, and quickly moved down street twenty feet just as a gunman hidden on the roof of a mercantile store fired three rapid shots from a rifle. The bullets thunked into the wooden walk where Vent and Sharp had been standing.

Across the street Borden tilted his shotgun upward and let off both barrels through the overhang. He laughed when the charges of double-ought buck ripped into the hidden gunman. Vent watched as the man's body rolled loosely down the side of the roof and fell into the dust of the alley.

Suddenly the street seemed to close down. No more shots pounded the night. No streaks of flame sought them out. One by one lights in the cantinas began going off until Borden called out, "The next man who turns off a light gets a load of buck up his butt."

The lights stayed on.

As Vent started along the street, a horse and rider burst from the alley leading to the livery stable and raced north. As the horse passed by a cantina, Vent saw the man was mounted on Arbuckle's stud.

"Coup, your stud," Vent called, and was answered by a half-crazed cross between a laugh and a snarl as the hunchback walked to where a horse lay dead in the street, cut down by the murderous crossfire. Leaning down, he jerked a rifle free with his good arm, lifted it and held it steady for a long moment. The gun roared and a spear of flame seemed to leap from the barrel and reach out the length of the town to slam the rider over the left shoulder of the stud and beneath its racing hooves.

"Come back here, you bastard!" Arbuckle shouted, and

the horse suddenly slid to a stop, whirled and came trotting back, its head high and its teeth bared.

Borden, who had just walked up, commented, "Should have let that feller go. He'd have been back in ten minutes. Now you're stuck with that damn brute."

Arbuckled giggled and went to retrieve his mount as it stepped gingerly around the still body of a man lying in the middle of the street.

Looking around, Vent became aware of dark faces peering from cantinas and doorways. Then a tall man wearing a sombrero came along the sidewalk, paused to glance down at the dead man draped over the edge of the water trough and moved on again. He stopped before Vent just as The Preacher, nursing a wounded arm, and Augustino, his hat on the back of his head, a cigar belching smoke from between white even teeth that shone behind the wide-stretched smiling mouth, came up and stood watching the stranger.

A badge gleamed from his chest and he wore two guns.

"You the marshal or the sheriff?" Vent asked.

"Sheriff," the man said. "Name's Cabel Dorton." He left it at that and Vent knew who he was and quickly inventoried his store of knowledge of this man, whose reputation had carried far beyond the south Colorado country he called home.

"Know who these fellers was?" Vent asked as Sharp and the others spread out like a fanned poker hand in a neat semicircle facing Dorton.

Watching them, Dorton smiled. "No need for that, boys. Just because I'm the sheriff, don't mean I'm a damn fool." Nodding toward the silent dead, he looked at Vent and said, "Drifted up from Texas two days ago. Said they worked for a combine. Said they was waiting for some cow thieves and killers . . . You boys cow thieves and killers?''

Borden chuckled. Sharp blew cigar smoke in the air and bemusedly watched it drift away on the night breeze. The half-crazed eyes of the hunchback gleamed wilder in the night and The Preacher nursed his wounded arm and contemplated the moon. Augustino moved restlessly and the bells on his California spurs tinkled softly.

''We've stolen cows and killed some fellers,'' Vent admitted.

A faint smile crossed the sheriff's face, making him look as if he were in deep concentration. ''Can't recall ever seeing a wanted dodger in my office. Reckon all I can do is buy you fellers a drink and wish you luck.''

''Doctor in this town?'' the Preacher asked, and Vent looked at him and saw the dark smear of blood on his left sleeve as the light from the cantina washed over them.

''Two blocks down and one to the right,'' Dorton said. He turned and called to a man standing on the edge of the sidewalk, ''Manuel, go fetch the body snatcher and a wagon and clean up this mess. Pick up what's left in Poco's too, will ya?''

The man called Manuel nodded, then said bitterly, ''Poco, he's dead. These fellows keel him inside when the big fight start.''

''Accident,'' Dorton said. ''Now go on. Get it done.''

''Sí, el Jefe,'' The Mexican said.

As he walked past Augustino, the Mexican gunfighter reached out and placed a hand on his sleeve and said in Spanish, ''Friend, we tried to warn him. But those others moved too fast. We do not kill innocent men and it was their bullets that sent him to Jesus.''

The Mexican looked at his countryman for a moment, then nodded and moved off.

Dorton led Vent and his companions into the nearest cantina, where they settled at two tables with their backs to the wall.

Vent looked at the sheriff, then down at his drink and said musingly, "So those fellers said they worked for a combine, huh?"

"That's what they said," Dorton agreed. "Said they came down from Texas. They was a hardcase bunch, but 'pears they was riding saddles made for better men."

"Well, somebody else's gonna wind up sittin' them," Sharp observed.

Dorton rolled a cigarette, lit it and blew smoke into the silence. "Mind telling me why a bunch of Texas waddies would come after you fellers?"

Augustino, his eternal smile plastered on his face, hoisted his tequila, took a drink, licked salt from the top of his thumb, lifted a lemon chunk and sucked on it, made a wry face and said dreamily, "Funny thing, Señor Sheriff, about Texacans. They always seem to go around looking for trouble. Always mix in where they're not welcome. Funny men, those Texacans."

The hunchback sat nursing his whiskey and staring at a slim dark-haired bar girl who stood leaning against the plank near a back door. Sensing his eyes on her, she turned, looked into those crazed orbs and shuddered, quickly glancing away. Arbuckle rose and walked over, tapped her on the arm. As she slowly turned back to stare at him fearfully, he nodded toward the back door, reached down, took her hand and led her from the room.

Vent, watching the byplay, shook his head and turned back to Dorton. "You know any of those fellers?"

"Nope, but I've heard of at least three of them."

Borden sat running a swab through the twin bores of the vicious-looking shotgun, his face filled with concentration, as Vent nodded. "Anybody I should know?"

"One feller said he was called Johnny Deuce," the sheriff said.

Sharp raised his head and smiled. "Wonder if we nailed him?"

"What'd he look like?" Borden asked.

"Somebody's choir boy," Dorton replied. "Had blond wavy hair, a real babyface and was built like a boy. The only thing about him different from most any other wet-eared yearlin' was the way he could use them guns of his'n and the mean streak he had."

Sharp nodded. "Heard of him. Tough kid."

"Well, he's riding a cloud tonight," Borden said off-handedly. "I blew him outa his boots out behind the café."

"Who else?" Vent asked.

"Bill Capehart and Dandy Jack Doolin, the feller they call the Arkansas Kid," Dorton told him.

"They sent somebody," Augustino said.

"Yep, they did do that," Sharp agreed.

"Graveyards filled with them lightweights," Borden grunted, and deftly reassembled his shotgun and holstered it.

The Preacher came in and sat down. His arm was bulky with bandage beneath his shirt-sleeve. He had left the arm out of his coat sleeve and now the sleeve dangled down his side like a homeless cloth waif.

"How bad?" Vent asked.

The Preacher shrugged. "I've had worse." Then he glanced at Vent's bloody side and said, "Your turn," and only then did Vent recall having been burned in the fight. Draining off his whiskey, he rose and went out.

Chapter Six

In the next two months Vent and his gunfighters struck the combine's holdings from Arizona up through Nevada and even rode the rails into Montana to hit at Jake Sunderman's holdings there. They ran off cattle, burned hay fields and barns, rustled horses and blew up two of Johnny Tombstone Morgan's sawmills. They robbed Leach's silver-mine shipments and blasted two of them into oblivion, leaving behind a trail of destruction that they knew would force the five members of the combine back to the States.

In October they rode into Dodge City. It was the first time Vent had been back to Kansas since the Hawks family had attacked his home, killed his two brothers and left him bullet-ripped and crippled in the dust of his own front yard.

He had stopped briefly at the old ranch house, its roof now crumbling and its windows long since stolen and carried away. Sitting his horse near the gate, he gazed at the past through hard eyes. It was here, in this lonely prairie grassland that the boy, Vent Torrey, had fallen to the feuding Hawkses' guns only to reappear in Colorado as the man Leatherhand, whose gun work had become legendary throughout the West.

Sharp pushed his horse forward, nodded at the warped and collapsing buildings and asked, "Your old home place?"

Vent nodded. Pointing to a spot halfway between the front gate, where they sat their horses, and the crumbling house, he said, "It was there my brother fell and I got this hand." He held up the leather-covered member and for just a moment felt a terrible regret at what had happened to him here in this desolate ranch yard. "They gunned my brother right out of the haymow door up there," he said, and pointed toward the barn.

Sharp had his look, as did the others, then Vent turned the Appaloosa and led them toward Dodge.

Riding down Front Street, the gunmen kept a wary eye on the side streets and narrow alleys leading away from the main drag. The Atchison, Topeka & Santa Fe railroad was a thin ribbon of steel on their left; it was this cross-tied roadbed that had brought the six men to the famous cowtown. Deak Hammer owned a piece of it and Vent decided it would be their next target.

As the group rode along the street, men turned to watch them pass. Some stared boldly while others had their quick look and then turned away to concentrate on something else. Vent smiled when he noted one well-dressed drummer wheel about and stand staring into the window of a women's clothing store at several store dummies decked out in dresses and other pieces of female clothing.

As they rode past Dog Kelly's saloon, a slightly built man wearing black clothing and sporting a tied-down holstered pistol came walking to the edge of the wooden sidewalk and stood teetering on his heels.

Seeing him there, Vent rode over and sat looking down into the cold gray eyes. "Howdy, Mr. Holiday. I trust you are seeing good times."

Holiday allowed himself a thin smile. "Mr. Torrey, you've come a long way since the day I patched you up and buried your brothers."

"I owe you for that," Vent said.

"Maybe someday you can return the favor, but until then, why don't you boys join me down at the Dodge House for a drink?"

Nodding toward the heavily armed gunmen quietly sitting their horses behind him, Vent asked, "You know these fellers?"

Holiday smiled frostily. "If I didn't, I'd be the only man in Kansas that held that distinction."

As Vent stepped off his horse, two men on the street saw the group confronting Holiday, unbuttoned their coats and spread out until one was in the street and the other against the wall of a shop.

"Friends of yours?" Vent asked, nodding at the approaching men.

Holiday glanced around and said, "Jim and Ed Masterson. Lawmen hereabouts. They work for Jack Bridges."

Arbuckle rode forward and started coolly at Holiday, who stared back just as cooly. "He's the marshal here?"

Ed Masterson, hearing the question, stopped ten feet away and said quietly, "That he is, Mr. Arbuckle. You have a problem with that?" and his hand dropped to dangle near the butt of a heavy .45.

Turning his half-crazed eyes on Masterson, the hunchback said mildly, "Mr. Marshal, I ain't got no quarrel with you, but it wouldn't take a whole hell of a lot to start one."

"Nobody's looking for a quarrel," Jim Masterson said, and Vent glanced at him and nodded.

"We did not come to your town seeking a fight, Mr. Masterson. We're on our own business and will be moving along come first light tomorrow."

Holiday turned then and there was irritation in his voice as he said, "I know Mr. Torrey. I also know his friends. These fellers ain't rowdies. They don't waste their time hoorahing towns. I've invited them for a drink. You're welcome to join us."

The brothers glanced at each other and then Jim said, "Much obliged." Looking pointedly at the men's weapons, he added, "We have a law here in Dodge. Handguns not allowed to be worn in public. If you boys will drop down to my office, I'll keep track of them for you."

Vent shook his head. "Sorry, Marshal. We'd like to abide by your laws, but we've got a few enemies who would probably be happy to hand over half of Kansas to catch us naked."

Holiday started at Jim Masterson, then said softly, "I told you Mr. Torrey was a friend. I'll be responsible for his and his friends' actions. That suit you?"

The Mastersons did not like it, but they nodded and fell in beside Holiday and Vent as they made their way to the Dodge House.

The men dismounted and then Borden and the hunchback gathered up the horses. "Livery still down there?" Borden asked.

"Still there," Holiday said, and led the way inside. As the heavily armed riders pushed through the swinging doors, men looked up from their drinks and slowly all conversation ebbed away.

As Vent started down the room, a tough-looking oldster wearing his pistol on his left side rose and stared at the Missourian. "Well, well," he said. "Here we got the last of the Torreys, come to Dodge. It's a long way from Crested Butte now, ain't it?"

Vent, looking into the man's washed-out blue eyes that still held the fierceness of a lifetime of sudden violence, stopped and grew still as the men behind him moved against the wall and waited. Holiday stepped to the bar and watched casually as the Mastersons moved out of the line of fire between Vent and the old man.

"There'll be no shooting, gentlemen," Jim Masterson said sharply, "unless I do it."

Vent ignored him. Letting his eyes wander over the old man's body, he settled on the right hand, noting, that only one finger remained, and suddenly recalled, as if he were there at that instant, the smashing roar of the shotgun as he leveled and fired at this man, blowing away his gun and part of his hand. "Hawks," he breathed.

"It's me," the old man said. "I'm still around, and I'll live long enough to see they lay you down with yore boots on."

"You keep talking that way, old man, and you won't live long enough to see anybody planted," Sharp observed, and he suddenly palmed up his gun and let it drop in line with Hawks's chest.

Hawks did not move. Instead he curled his lip disdainfully and asked Vent, "This feller doing your dirty work for you now?"

Vent smiled. "Nope. He's just thirsty and you're interfering with his drinking."

"Then let him shoot or put that thing away," Hawks snapped.

Borden, who had slipped quietly through the door, followed by the hunchback, stepped around Vent and walked down the room. He stopped five feet from Hawks and looked into his eyes, then said without turning his head, "This here gent's defanged. He ain't gonna do nothing," and turned toward the bar and ordered a bottle and glasses.

Hawks's eyes flared with a sudden brilliance that was so intense Vent was sure he was going for his gun, but then he turned and walked to the back door, where he stopped, looked over his shoulder and said, "You should have killed me when you had the chance, Torrey," and he was gone.

"Now that's one hard old man," Sharp observed.

As they settled at a table in the rear of the room, a husky man dressed in a townsman's suit came in, pushed his hat to the back of his head and went to the bar, ignoring Vent and his friends.

"Jack Bridges," Augustino said softly, as the famous Kansas gunfighter accepted a drink from the bartender, picked it up with his left hand and quickly gulped it down, then replaced the glass on the bar top with exaggerated care.

Vent watched him with seeming indifference, but he had heard about this man and his strange sense of humor. They said of Bridges that you never knew whether he was serious or just joshing you, but when he went for his gun in earnest, there was no doubt of his intentions. He was snake-fast and absolutely merciless.

Now he suddenly whirled and slapped a hand to his gun butt. Six weapons appeared as if by magic in the hands of

Vent and his gunmen and the cocking of their hammers was loud in the stillness of the Dodge House.

Grinning, Bridges removed his hand from his gun and doffed his hat. "Gentlemen, welcome to the Dodge House, the finest hall of its kind this side of St. Louis and a place of refinement and genteel people. It is no place to shed blood; besides, shooting folks ruins my appetite for likker, a great deal of which I plan to consume this day."

Laughs greeted this sally from around the room and guns were reholstered as the Mastersons waved the marshal over and invited him to join them. Staring at him sourly, Holiday observed, "Someday, Jack, that sense of humor of yours is going to get you salivated."

Bridges grinned. "Probably," he agreed and raised his glass.

"Here's to a tight cinch and a handful of aces," he said, and tossed it off.

The others joined him.

Glancing at The Preacher, Bridges asked, "How long's it been, Preacher?"

"Ten years, I reckon," The Preacher answered.

Vent hadn't known the old gunfighter knew Bridges, but then thinking about it he figured the gambler probably knew half the famous pistol fighters in the West.

It turned out that the hunchback also knew Bridges, as did Sharp, who had once played keno in Dog Kelly's saloon during a cold Kansas winter when the players came to the table dressed in overcoats, blankets and with scarves tied around their ears. They had burned everything wooden that could be found in the town and had even torn down several corrals for their rails and posts, staking the horses out or keeping them tied up in lean-tos.

"It was so damn cold that winter ice froze on the

railroad track, and when the train came in, it skidded five miles west of town before the engineer could get it stopped,'' Sharp said with a straight face.

"I remember that winter," Bridges said. "It was so danged cold the cattle had to be wrapped in cowhide to keep them from falling apart."

While the men told their jokes and sipped their drinks, Vent glanced at the hunchback and nodded toward the back door. Rising, Arbuckle quietly left the table and moved to the back of the room and outside. Bridges, still telling jokes, watched the hunchback leave, then casually winding up a story, rose and said, "Pee call," and followed Arbuckle out.

Sharp looked at Vent, and he too rose and, remarking how "that wasn't a bad idea," followed Bridges.

Staring after them, Jim Masterson said, "If this keeps up, that old two-holer out there's gonna be pretty crowded."

Half an hour later, Arbuckle came in the front door, slid into a chair next to Vent, and poured himself a drink. "A whole passel of horses down at the stable. Looks like they been rid hard," he said.

Then Sharp came in the back door, followed closely by Bridges; he glanced at Vent, tilted his chin and walked to the bar. Vent rose and came over and Holiday, watching the byplay, poured another drink and looked sharply at the Mastersons.

"You boys running a little sandy, are ya?" the gray-eyed gambler asked. There was a casualness to the question that might have put some men off, but the Mastersons knew Holiday and neither one of them wanted to gain the enmity of this cadaverous gunman who was dying of lung fever and whose explosive temperment and swift draw were legendary.

Vent had overheard the question and now he turned and watched the two brothers, wondering if they were part of this. He knew what those horses signified.

"You read their brands?" Vent asked the hunchback.

"Montana and Texas," Arbuckle said.

Bridges leaned on the bar, turning his glass slowly in his slim hand, then looked at Vent and there was no banter in the tone as he asked, "You boys got troubles?"

"A little run-in with some gents from Texas," Vent said.

"Couldn't be that they work for Leach and his friends, could they?" Bridges asked.

Before Vent could answer, he heard Ed Masterson say, "We ain't setting anybody up. We just want this town to stay quiet and with six of the most widely known men on both sides of the Rockies in town, it just don't seem possible that that'll happen."

Holiday lifted his drink and tossed it off, then said calmly, "You fellers plan to interfere with that bunch you better go over to Tom Sundry's laying-out parlor and arrange for a couple of coffins 'cause you'll need 'em."

"We don't aim to butt into their business as long as they keep it this side the track, but the first man who crosses over into Maple, I'll shoot him," Masterson promised.

Holiday looked up, caught Vent's eyes on the table and smiled faintly. "You boys are pretty good, but they ain't a man in that bunch who couldn't spot you two seconds and beat you to it."

Vent turned then and Sharp said, "I figure they got the livery boxed. If we move down there for our horses, it'll be fight or die."

Ed Masterson rose and came over and stood in front of

Vent. "Mr. Torrey, I've heard you're a fair man. I want to know what we're bucking here."

Vent nodded. "That's putting it square. I'll answer you. We got us a little war going with Deak Hammer, Stiles Leach, Amos Dewberry, Johnny Morgan and Jake Sunderman. They kidnapped my sister. If you are a gentleman, you'll not interfere in this. In most places, those men would swing for that."

"And if they had done it here, they would have wound up doing the hemp fandango on our new scaffold, big guns or no," Masterson said.

"I believe that," Vent replied. "If you can show us how to get our horses, we'll take our fight with these hired guns somewhere else."

Bridges grinned and, turning to the bartender, said, "Willie, toss me your Greener," and the apron brought up a sawed-off shotgun from beneath the bar and handed it to the marshal. Breaking it, he looked at the twin shells, then held out his hand and the bartender filled it with more shells from a box. Stuffing his pockets with the heavy double-ought buck rounds, he nodded at the door and said, "Ed, get Jim and let's meander down there and invite those boys to leave town."

As the Mastersons flanked Bridges, Holiday rose and joined them.

"Not your fight, Doc," Bridges said.

"It is now," Holiday grunted, and they left.

Vent nursed his drink and waited, wondering if the visiting gunmen would leave or show fight. He knew that if they chose to go to the gun, he would lead his men into the street and side the law.

Twenty minutes passed as the second hand on Slab Borden's big old railroad watch dragged itself around the dial, then the doors swung open and Bridges came in, followed by the Mastersons. Strolling up to the bar, he slid the shotgun to the bartender and said with a grin, "Thanks, Willie." Turning to Vent, he jerked his head toward the street. "They decided Dodge City just wasn't their cup of tea."

Vent nodded. "Thanks. Mind telling me which way they went?"

Ed Masterson came up then, waited until the bartender poured his drink, tossed it off and, making a face, said, "They were traveling east the last we saw of them, but that don't mean they kept on going in that direction."

Bridges looked at Ed Masterson and back at Vent. "The feller ramrodding that bunch was Tonto McCord."

"Jake Sunderman's gun," Arbuckle grunted.

"Heard he was fast," Sharp said.

Slab Borden looked sour as he shifted the heavy shotgun to a more comfortable place on his hip. "He's fair, but no match for any man here."

"I recognized a couple of those boys," Jim Masterson said. "One of them was Ben Cravens."

Vent had heard of Cravens. He was a young outlaw who had taken to rustling and killing when just a boy and had built a reputation for gun handling around Oklahoma and eastern Texas.

Looking at The Preacher, Vent observed, "It seems to me these big-money boys have taken to digging up a few fellers with big reps and sending them out heading up a bunch of Texas gunnies. I think maybe it's time to cure them of that habit."

Later that day, Vent and his fellow gunmen got the chance. Riding west along the Atchison, Topeka & Santa Fe line, they stopped their horses on a small rise in the plains to blow and suddenly Borden raised a massive arm and pointed toward where the track dipped into a hollow about half a mile west.

"Well, I'll be damned," Vent said as he watched a large group of riders leading their horses up a ramp and into three box cars while the train puffed black smoke into the sky and idled its steam away.

"There's our Texas waddies." Sharp grinned.

Carefully examining the land around them, Vent noticed a shallow cut in the prairie leading away from their position in a wide swing that curved back to just north of where the train sat. "Figure that cut's deep enough to hide us?" he asked, and the gunmen turned and looked at it.

The Preacher grinned his hard grin and said softly, "Yep, and if we hurry we should come up on that train in plenty of time to catch those boys flatfooted."

Arbuckle looked at Vent. "You got some kinda plan working?"

"We're gonna wait until those boys are inside the cars, then we're just gonna ride on up and slam the doors on them." Vent grinned.

Watching Sharp, Vent could see the wheels turning. "Then we take over the train and run it on west until we find a nice place to ditch those fellers," he said.

Borden growled, "Why not just bump them off?"

"Like shooting fish in a rain barrel," the hunchback said softly, his eyes glittering at the thought.

"Killing those fellers would scare hell outa everybody, but it would also put every sheriff and lawman in the West on us," Vent said.

In spite of his reputation for wildness, Arbuckle had a vein of practicality in his makeup and now he said, "I agree with Vent. Better way to do it is make damn fools outa them.''

Augustino pushed his horse forward, had his look, and, perpetual smile in place, said, ''They're about loaded, *amigos*. Hadn't we better vamos?''

Bending low in their saddles, the six gunmen rode along the depression until they were opposite the train. Vent grinned when he saw there were no openings in the box cars. Lifting his chin toward the front of the train, he said, ''Owney, you and The Preacher want to sorta ride on up there and relieve the engineer?''

''Our pleasure,'' Sharp replied, goosed his horse up the bank and rode leisurely across the prairie, followed by the tall black-clad figure of The Preacher, who rode bolt upright. Watching the two dark-clothed figures, Vent thought, Yesterday and today . . . and then wondered where he fit, finally deciding it really didn't matter.

Grunting ''Let's go,'' he led the others up the bank and straight to the side of the track. Dismounting, they tied their horses to the side of the box cars and carefully circled between them, sliding over the turnbuckles and peeping around the edge of the cars. A pair of legs dangled from the first car and Vent could hear the stomp and shuffle of horses coming from there; he figured probably one or two men were riding with the mounts while the others were taking their ease in the remaining box cars. Carefully examining the doors, he noted that if a door was shoved hard along its track, it would seat itself, and all a man would have to do would be to slam the locking mechanism over and he'd have himself a carful of prisoners.

At a nod Borden moved behind the first and second car, then crawled over the turnbuckle of the last car and took up station by the door. Augustino made his way to the second door and Arbuckle placed a hand on the third door and looked back at Vent, waiting for his signal. Stepping into the open where the man sitting in the door of the last car could see him, Vent drew his .44, leveled it on the man's chest and said softly, "Back inside, friend." He watched the man's eyes grow round with consternation. Then the man quickly turned on his butt and rolled from view, and Vent called "Now," and watched with satisfaction as the heavy doors were rolled simultaneously along their tracks and locked shut.

"Hey, what the hell's going on out there?" someone shouted.

Borden laughed and, standing near the door, shouted, "You fellers looking for Leatherhand and his friends?"

"Dammit, open this here door," a hard voice called.

"That you, Tonto?" Arbuckle called.

"Yore damned right it's me," came McCord's gravelly voice, and then a shot boomed from inside the car and a hole suddenly appeared in the door. The bullet missed Borden by less than six inches.

"Try that again and we'll pump these cars so full of lead the train won't be able to move them," the hunchback threatened.

There were no more shots.

Gathering up the horses, Vent opened the last car in the line, lowered its loading ramp and led the animals aboard. Arbuckle's stud snorted and bared its teeth until the hunchback shouted at it to behave. Rolling its eyes wildly, it entered the car, biting at Vent's Appy as it passed up the ramp, only to receive a sharp kick in the chest for its efforts.

"Damn stud," Arbuckle grunted.

Once the horses were loaded Vent walked down to

where the Preacher and Sharp held their guns on the engineer and his fireman.

"You fellers willing to behave?" Vent asked.

"What the hell's going on here?" the engineer snapped.

"Why nothing much," Vent told him. "We're just gonna borrow your train for a while. Now you can either pilot her or we'll put you off right here and you can walk back to Dodge."

Staring at him, the fireman protested, "Hell, man, that's a good ten miles. In this heat a feller might just not make it."

"Oh, you'll make it, all right," Vent assured him. "Me, I once walked over a hundred miles in August down in Arizona. All the way from the Verde Valley to Dry Springs. You'll make her."

The engineer looked out at the flat expanse of prairie that reached all the way to the horizon without a break, and shook his head. He did not like Kansas. He did not like any country where there were no mountains, creeks or trees. He had been born in the Appalachian Mountains and had never gotten used to this desolate land filled with violence and danger. If it wasn't Indians scalping and killing folks, it was gunmen and outlaws like these three men who faced him, forcing a man to do things he didn't want to do at pistol point. Vent could see the man's hesitation working at him and said quietly, "We got no quarrel with you, mister. They's two box cars full of gunnies back there out to kill us. It's them we're interested in, not you. You do what you're told and we'll get along fine."

Shrugging, the engineer took out a plug of tobacco, bit off a chew and offered the plug to Vent, who shook his head. Sharp and The Preacher also turned it down. Dropping the tobacco in his pocket, he said, "You say when," and placed his hand on the throttle, preparatory to getting up a good head of steam.

"Let her flicker whenever you're ready," Vent said, and, leaving Sharp to watch over his charges, dropped from the train and moved along the track to the last car. Clambering aboard, he glanced at Arbuckle, who was cursing the big stud, and said, "Maybe a couple of you fellers ought to climb up on top of them two cars and kinda keep an eye out. Those fellers just might try to climb out through an air vent."

Borden and the hunchback left the car, dropping to the ground just as the train began to move. Vent grinned at the Mexican and said, "I'm going up front. Keep an eye out back here, huh, Angel?"

As Vent trotted alongside the slowly moving train, Arbuckle and Borden climbed a ladder up the side of the second car and Borden sat down near the vent of the second car while Arbuckle moved on to take up a position just behind the second vent.

Overtaking the engine, Vent swung aboard and said, "Just keep her rolling until I tell you to stop," and the engineer nodded.

The train rolled west, passing through Cimarron without stopping, which set the telegrapher's keys to rattling all up and down the line from Wichita to Las Animas. As the sun slipped below the horizon, Vent asked the engineer, "How much further before we have to take on water?"

"Should have filled her up back at Cimarron, but I reckon she'll make Pierceville."

They arrived at the scattering of shacks that was Pierceville just after midnight and Vent climbed stiffly from the cab, followed by the Preacher, who stood by while the fireman climbed the water tower and swung the canvas pipe into place. Turning on the lever, he stood stolidly by while the precious fluid poured into the boiler tank. Several men standing on the platform watched silently as Borden and Arbuckle climbed down off the top of the cars and stepped up on the wooden deck fronting the station.

Borden, hands on hips, asked, "They a place to eat in this here burg?"

One of the men standing near the train looked up and said, "I own a café down the street."

Pointing to where Vent was standing near the rear of the train, the big man said, "See that feller down there? Well, you fetch us some food and he'll pay you. We'll need about forty sandwiches, a couple dozen airtights of peaches, about twenty gallons of coffee, half a dozen loaves of bread and twenty pies. Can you handle that?"

Staring at Borden, the café owner said wonderingly, "Mister, you're a hell of a big feller, but even you can't eat that much."

"Ain't fer me; leastways, part of it ain't," Borden growled.

"Well, I guess I can fix you up, but it'll sure as hell empty my larder," the man complained.

"You'll be paid," Borden grunted. "Now git at it."

After the man went away Borden pointed to another man who was standing beneath the station lantern and snapped, "You, get a couple of buckets and start toting water down to those last two cars and hunt up some tin cups."

Stepping into the light, the man said softly, "Now just who the hell are you to order me around?"

"I'm the gent that's going to fill yore guts full of

buckshot if you don't git going,'' Borden snarled as another man came up and took the first man's sleeve.

Urging him away, the second man muttered, ''That there's Slab Borden, man. You wanta get killed?''

''The hell he is?'' the first man marveled as he disappeared inside the station.

The food arrived at the same time the fireman rehung the hose and shut off the water. Vent, meanwhile, had called to McCord and received his guarantee there would be no gunplay if doors were opened and food and water passed inside.

''What about our horses?'' McCord called.

''We'll off-load 'em and see they're watered,'' Vent promised.

An hour later, the horses watered and the men fed, Vent shoved the doors closed and locked them as McCord and several of his Texas gunfighters cursed bitterly. The train rolled out. Swinging aboard, Vent leaned against the side of the rocking engine and hungrily wolfed two huge beef sandwiches, a slice of apple pie and half a can of peaches, washing it down with four cups of strong black coffee.

It was just breaking day when the train, pouring smoke from its bell stack, approached Holcomb. The Preacher moved back beside Vent and, touching his arm lightly, awoke him from a half-sleeping, half-awake condition. ''Town coming up,'' he said, pointing ahead.

''That'll be Holcomb.'' The Missourian leaned out to watch the station move toward them. The station master was standing on the platform holding a flag in his right hand. ''What's the flag for?'' Vent asked the engineer.

''Wants me to stop,'' the engineer said.

''Any reason why?''

"Probably got some mail . . ."

Vent watched as the man at first waved his flag casually, then, as the train bore down on him without slackening speed, more vigorously, pointing as he did at a mailbag hanging from a nail in the station wall. As Vent watched, a gunshot sounded and the flagpole suddenly snapped, sending the flag one way and a frightened station master the other. Leaning far out the window, Vent looked back and was in time to see the sun flicker off a falling shell casing as the hunchback punched out his empty and replaced it with a live round.

"Funny sense of humor," The Preacher observed.

Five miles west of Holcomb Vent found what he had been looking for. The track spanned a deep ravine held up by wooden trestle timbers that looked like a thousand jigsaw puzzles entangled in a free-for-all.

"Stop on this side of the trestle," Vent ordered, and the engineer pulled back on the throttle and hit the brake lever, bringing the short-coupled train to a halt twenty feet out on the bridge. Cursing, he applied steam and backed the engine off the trestle, bringing it to a halt two engine lengths from the ravine edge.

"That's just fine," Vent said, and pointed back along the track toward Holcomb. "You and your fireman can start back. The walk isn't that much. We'll take it from here."

"What you fellers gonna do with my engine?" the man asked, but his face showed he already knew.

"Not to worry," The Preacher advised. "Trust in the Lord, my friend, and move along now."

As the engineer and his fireman trudged east along the right-of-way, Vent went back and opened the car doors, dropped the loading ramps and led the horses onto the prairie, where Arbuckle's stud immediately fell to its knees preparatory to rolling over and crushing the hunchback's saddle in the process.

"Damn ornery beast," Arbuckle shouted; he whipped out his gun and fired, putting a bullet through the animal's right ear. Snorting wildly, the horse sprang to its feet and ran fifty feet out in the prairie where it stood flicking its injured ear back and forth and snorting.

Augustino, smiling, went to his own mount, removed the saddle and led him away from the car, where he allowed him to roll until he was satisfied, then resaddled and tied the animal to one of the cars.

While this byplay was going on, Vent, assisted by Borden and Sharp, unloaded McCord's men's horses and off-saddled them. Once they were stripped, he tied them head to tail in a long packer's string and left Borden to take care of them.

A voice suddenly came from inside the first car and Vent walked over and waited while McCord called, "What the hell you fellers doing out there?"

"Fixing to set the cars on fire," Arbuckle told him, laughing and giggling in his high falsetto. In spite of himself Vent felt the hair rise on his scalp and somehow knew that if it had been left up to the hunchback, that is exactly what he would have done.

"By God, you wouldn't do that . . . would you?" McCord said, his voice filled with apprehension. Apparently he had recognized Arbuckle's voice and knew the hunchback was capable of anything, including burning thirty men to death.

"Not this time, McCord," Vent said, and walked away. Standing at the edge of the ravine, he was joined by Borden and Augustino, leaving Arbuckle at the cars where he was taking great delight in taunting the incarcerated victims with threats of firing into the cars through the walls or allowing them to fall off the track into the ravine.

The Preacher came up and, glancing back at Arbuckle, observed, "That feller sometimes gives me the willies."

Borden looked at The Preacher, then grinned. "They say he once cut out a feller's liver and ate it raw."

His face expressionless, The Preacher mused, "Wonder why he didn't cook it?"

Pointing down into the ravine, Vent said, "Slab, you reckon you could blow that bridge with the stuff you got left?"

"Well, we used up almost the last of it on that silver mine, but I got ten sticks and if I plant them just right, it'll come down."

Vent nodded. "Go to it," he said, and went back and off-saddled the Appy and allowed him to roll, then gave him a rubdown with handfuls of grass.

Half an hour later Borden clambered up the bank from the bottom of the ravine and announced that the explosives were in place. In his huge fist he held the end of a long fuse; he fired up a cigar and, looking at Vent, waited.

"Hold the horses, will you, Coup?" Vent asked, and the hunchback caught up the animals and led them to the rear of the cars, where he waited, half-crazed eyes gleaming with anticipation. He had told the imprisoned men the plan was to blow up the cars with them inside.

Borden touched his cigar to the fuse and walked back to stand close to the engine. Vent stood behind him, waiting. When the explosive went off, timbers and large beams were hurled into the air, followed by a column of dust that reached a height of a hundred feet, only to be whipped away on the prairie winds.

The bridge seemed to hang in midair for long seconds, then slowly crumpled into the ravine, where it caught fire from flames set off by the dynamite.

Climbing into the cab of the uncoupled engine, Vent began building up a head of steam until black smoke was boiling from the stack, blending with the smoke from the burning bridge. Then he shoved the throttle forward and dropped off. The train picked up speed, then suddenly reached the edge of the shattered trestle, where its cow catcher dropped nose over, leaving the engine hanging almost in midair for a long moment before it fell into the wreckage and the boiler exploded.

Inside the two box cars men began shouting questions and cursing wildly as the acrid smell of smoke bit at their nostrils. Walking back, Vent called, ''McCord, you hear me?''

''I hear you,'' McCord answered, then began coughing as smoke swirled up beneath the car, penetrating the cracks in the floor.

''I'm fixing to open the doors. You fellers toss out your guns and then come out five at a time with your dew claws on top of yore hats. The man who doesn't follow orders gets salivated.''

''All right, you sonofabitch!'' McCord shouted. Vent directed Borden and Arbuckle to the top of the two cars, slid back the doors, prudently standing clear of a possible leaden ambush from inside, and waited as the men filed out five at a time, were carefully searched for holdout guns, then marched to the embankment just off the right-of-way and made to sit with their hands still on top of their heads.

Looking them over, The Preacher said, ''Scrapings from

the bottom of the barrel, Vent. We shoulda probably let 'em fry in there.''

Overhearing the remark, one of the Texans snarled, ''I don't know who you are, mister, but you give me a gun and face me alone and I'll show you who the hell came from the bottom of the barrel.''

Grinning, The Preacher walked over, said, ''Stand up,'' and, when the man was on his feet, ordered, ''Walk over there by the box car.''

When the man had taken his stance, The Preacher called, ''Angel, *amigo,* loan this mouth one of your hoglegs.'' He watched as the Mexican walked over and slipped one of his fancy guns into the Texan's holster. Looking back at The Preacher, Augustino said, ''Please be careful, *compadre,* and do not hit the pistolo by accident. It is one of a pair, you know.''

Vent looked at the man and said, ''You know who this gent is?''

''No, and I don't give a damn,'' the Texan snarled.

''Plug the bastard,'' one of his friends called from the embankment.

McCord spoke up then. ''Hey, Billy, where you want your body sent?''

''You figure that old wornout hombre's gonna beat me?'' the Texan asked in wonder.

''He sure as hell is,'' McCord said. ''That's The Preacher you're about to swap lead with.''

Vent watched the color drain from the man's face as he realized where his mouth had put him. ''You want out of this you say so,'' he told him, and watched the emotions cross the man's face like soldiers of doubt all in a row. Finally, the man growled, ''I can't no way beat you, mister, but I reckon I let my big mouth buy this, so let her flicker. I'll take my medicine like a good little damn fool.''

A gleam of admiration for the man touched The Preacher's eyes, then he drew like lightning and fired; the man grunted, raised a hand to his chest and pawed feebly at the terrible hurt there. Collapsing against the side of the car, he slid down its wooden side, hit the ground and rolled over. Gasping in agony, he drew his knees far up into his chest, then kicked them out and dug his bootheels into the dirt.

''Damn you,'' one of the men said, and The Preacher turned and fastened his clear brittle eyes on the man. He spoke so softly Vent barely heard him above the retching of the dying Texan. ''You can go hold his hand on the trail to hell, my friend.''

The Texan suddenly stiffened, then seemed to fall into himself as his mouth dropped open and blood poured down into his dirty white scarf, turning it red.

''He had his chance,'' Vent said. ''He knew nobody was going to coax him. He chose it, he bought it,'' and he turned away as the body relaxed in death. Stopping to look down into the dead face, he said almost to himself, ''They never look like much when the life's gone. . . .''

Looking at Tonto McCord then, Vent saw there the sudden realization of what he was into, what the combine, in their reach for a new gambling thrill, had caused, and it was obvious he did not like it.

Walking over to him, Vent said, ''You should have told these boys who they were bucking.''

One of the Texans looked up and said sourly, ''What the hell was there to worry about? An old man, a cripple with a leather hand, a Mex who spent more for his clothes than he did for food, a hunchback and a giant who would rather ride a mule than a horse, like other men.''

A skinny Texan with a walrus mustache, whose lined face showed he had spent his share of hard winters and long summers, said bitterly, "You forgot to mention the duded-up gambling man with the you-all talk. Hell, he don't look like much either."

McCord looked at them and said sarcastically, "And thirty men let six waddies outthink them and then buffalo them."

"You were one of the thirty," the skinny rider pointed out.

McCord's jaw muscles bunched, but he didn't answer.

Vent and his men mounted up and, leading the Texans' horses, rode north, leaving behind a group of men whose high heels would wear blisters on their feet long before they reached Holcomb. They would also be wiser. The horses were off-saddled five hours later and released and the saddles stacked near the trail.

Four days later Vent and his wornout riders camped at Sharon Springs beneath a tall stand of cottonwoods that gave shade to a rough-looking building where the stage stopped every fourth day to change horses on its long run into Colorado.

Vent looked the place over as they rode in and noted but one horse tied to the hitch rack in front of the wide verandah. The structure itself was a good seventy-five feet long and fifty feet deep. A second floor furnished rooms to weary travelers who either stopped on their way west or laid over when the stage rolled into the place at night.

After the horses were watered and off-saddled, each man staked his mount out in a field north of the stage stop but within easy reach of the camp spot. As usual Arbuckle's stud was left to wander on its own.

The six men walked across the hard-packed yard in front

of the station and stepped up on the verandah just as a man dressed in a pair of Levi's, a rough denim jacket and a battered Stetson that had once been white, came through the door. He wore a heavy pair of bullhide chaps and a single handgun thrust into a chap pocket within easy reach of his dangling right hand.

Nodding as he passed, he said, "If you boys are heading west, better put scouts out and watch the cutbanks. Indians damned near lifted my hair near Cheyenne Wells."

Vent thanked him, then asked, "You recognize the tribe?"

"Couldn't tell," the rider admitted ruefully. "I was covering ground so fast I wouldn't have recognized old General Sherman if he was on my tail." He tramped out to his horse and mounted, then rode up to the verandah and said quietly, "Mr. Leatherhead, you don't know me, but you once did a favor for my brother so I figure I owe you. They's ten riders came through here yesterday and they asked old Sod Jenkins in there a hell of a lot of questions and all of them were about you fellers. One of them's still here. Seems his horse went lame . . . or maybe he's waiting to spy out you boys. His pony's around back and he's inside getting likkered up."

"Much obliged, friend," Vent said. "Now I owe you one."

"Just so," the man said, and, turning his horse, rode east at a fast trot.

Glancing at Sharp, Vent thought a moment, then said, "This feller's gonna be lookin' for six riders. What if we give him one?"

Arbuckle grinned. "Think he'll talk a little more easily if just one man comes in?"

"It hangs on whether he knows we rode in here," Vent

replied. "If he's drunk or even half drunk, there's a good chance he's been too busy drinking to notice us."

"I take it you want me to go in?" Sharp said.

"Probably be best, Owney. The rest of us sorta stand out in a crowd. . . ."

Sharp smiled as he looked from one man to the other, then wordlessly pushed open the swinging doors and disappeared.

As Sharp came in from the bright sunlight to the dark cavern of the combination saloon and mercantile, he stepped quickly to the left of the door, not liking the idea of being backlighted against the outside, and stood for the few seconds it required for his eyes to adjust to the light. Walking down the room he stepped up to the bar, leaning his elbows on the plank near where a solidly built man wearing town clothes, topped off by a bowler hat with the rim rolled up, stood nursing a bottle and glass.

Turning, the man said, "Howdy, stranger. Belly up and join the festivities. The whiskey tastes like it was distilled in a glue factory and the beer's so flat you can take a sighting on it, but it's all old Sod's got so reckon you'll have to suffer along with me."

Nodding his thanks, Sharp raised the freshly poured drink and tossed it down; suddenly his eyes bulged and he clutched his throat, choking. "My God, I've been poisoned!"

Grinning, the drinker said, "See what I mean. Ain't it some shakin's though. When Sod here says his likker's hard, he ain't kiddin'. It's hard all right . . . hard to stomach," and the man threw back his head and laughed.

Sod Jenkins was a bear of a man with shoulders almost as broad as Slab Borden's. His huge hands lay on the plank now, but Sharp had heard they could break a man's back or tear off an arm; he thought about how many rounds it would take to stop this man and hoped he'd not have to find out.

"You mind pouring me one of those flat beers to sort of chase this stuff," he said. "Me, I ain't used to drinking furniture polish in place of whiskey."

"My name's Broke Blankinship," the drinker introduced himself.

Sharp shook hands, said, "I'm Al Jones," and picked up the beer; he swallowed a mouthful and decided Blankinship was right. It was flat enough to spread. "Got anything around here to eat?" he asked.

"Big pot of chili back there." Jenkins jerked his chin toward an ancient stove near the end of the backbar, its top covered with pots and pans.

"Don't try it unless you got a copper-riveted gut," Blankinship warned. "That stuff'll eat the bluing right offin' yore gun barrel."

"It's mighty tasty when you dip her up with a tortilla," Jenkins protested.

"I'll try anything once," Sharp said. Blankinship turned then and brushed back his coat, dug out a couple of cigars. The gambler noted the heavy shell belt he wore under his coat and wondered just how drunk this man was.

"You just ride in from the east?" Blankinship asked casually, handing Sharp a cigar and lighting it for him.

"Yep, been over to Hays bucking the tiger," Sharp said, and drew on the cigar. It was a good one and had cost the man at least a half dollar; he wondered why Blankinship was called "Broke."

He decided to ask. "How come they call you Broke?"

Blankinship grinned. "Reckon it's 'cause I got me this damn fool habit of always going for broke. If it's gambling, women or fighting, I always seem to carry her right to the corral fence.''

''Feller can build some scars that way,'' Sharp observed.

''He either gets good or he gets gone.'' Blankinship tossed off his fifth drink since Sharp had entered the saloon.

Jenkins brought the chili and sided it with a pile of tortillas and small green chili peppers. After one taste of the chili, Sharp gasped for breath and his face suddenly poured sweat.

Grinning, Blankinship said, ''I told you that stuff was pure dynamite. Hell, old Sod here, he uses it to blow stumps and rocks off his land when he ain't feeding it to some poor damn pilgrim.''

Sharp took another bite and this time managed to get it down with at least part of his windpipe intact. ''Whew, that stuff's hot enough to burn holes in a water trough,'' he observed.

''Probably drop right through and into yore boots,'' Blankinship said, then sobering, asked, ''See any Injuns?''

''Nope, didn't see anything except a few fellers on horseback and a wagon train going west.''

''You want some more of that chili?'' Jenkins asked, and Sharp looked down and was surprised he had actually cleaned up the bowl.

''Thanks anyway,'' he said, ''but I don't reckon I'll starve now, although I may never be able to eat again.''

Blankinship, his face serious, said, ''Don't worry about it, friend. For the next year or so that stuff'll just lay down there and eat up anything you put down with it. Best little digester ever invented . . . You say you saw riders?''

''Yeah.'' Sharp nodded and took a puff on his cigar.

"I'm expecting some friends . . . several fellers on their way to Denver. Waiting to ride on through with them . . ."

"I saw half a dozen riders over near Page City," Sharp said.

"Was one of them a tall feller wearing a leather glove on his gun hand?"

Glancing at Jenkins, Sharp saw the man's eyes suddenly narrow, and thought, He knows who Vent is. Affecting a casual tone, he said, "Come to think on it, they was a gent with a leather contraption on his hand. Some other fellers was with him. One of 'em rode a black mule and carried a shotgun in a hip holster. Never saw a man do that before."

Jenkins apparently lost interest. He wandered off and was working down at the far end of the bar when Sharp casually drew his gun, aligned it on Blankinship's stomach and said, "Fact is, them fellers you was interested in is right outside that front door."

Blankinship looked down at the .45, then up into Sharp's eyes and said disgustedly, "You'll be Owney Sharp, right?"

"Well, I sure as hell ain't Al Jones. . . ."

"You gonna use that?" Blankinship glanced down at the pistol again.

"Depends on you," Sharp told him.

Jenkins looked back from the head of the bar. "You fellers want anything just holler."

"Might need a gravedigger if Mr. Blankinship here don't start talking to me," Sharp said, and Jenkins suddenly stiffened and started to drop his hands beneath the counter when the back door opened and Slab Borden came in behind his shotgun, held hip high and rock steady, its gaping bores perfectly aligned with Jenkins's face.

Borden was followed by Vent, Arbuckle and The Preacher. They walked calmly to the bar and, nodding at Sharp, called for drinks. Jenkins, his hands steady in spite of his obvious fright, set up a bottle and glasses, then Borden, raising the tip of the shotgun a scant inch in salute, said, "Better bring me a bottle while you're at it."

Jenkins served him and couldn't seem to keep his eyes off the shotgun bores.

Vent, drink in hand, strolled down the bar, stopped just behind Blankinship and asked Sharp, "This feller say who he is?"

"This gentleman's name is Broke Blankinship and according to the way he tells it, he's a man who always goes for broke."

"That so?"

Blankinship turned carefully, keeping his hands high and away from his waist, and said, "You'll be Leatherhand."

"Guilty," Vent agreed. "You got a case of the curiosities, Mr. Blankinship?"

"Just doing what I been paid for," Blankinship said sourly.

"Hope it's enough to pay for a funeral," Arbuckle grunted. "Why don't you fellers just leave this here gent to me." Blankinship had his look at those half-crazed eyes and decided he'd rather be under Sharp's gun than facing the hunchback. Vent could see it written across his face as Blankinship stared at Arbuckle with new fear in his eyes.

"Looks like Mr. Blankinship has heard a few things about you, Coup," The Preacher observed mildly, then suddenly backhanded Blankinship, knocking him off his feet.

The man hit the floor solidly and, whipping back his coat, dropped a hand to his gun butt, then froze as The Preacher drew so swiftly it looked like the gun had been there from the beginning. Looking sick, Blankinship slowly removed his hand from his gun and said, ''I reckon I'll just stay down here. No use getting up to get knocked down again.''

Vent smiled. He was beginning to like the man's nerve. ''Which one of the combine you working for, Mr. Blankinship?''

''Morgan,'' he answered without hesitation.

''He tell you what's happening here?''

Blankinship looked up at Vent, then let his eyes travel from face to face. ''Seems to me almost everybody between St. Louis and Tombstone, Arizona, has heard about this deal. A few have even heard about Leach having your sister kidnapped.''

Curious now, Vent asked, ''Why would a man like you, Mr. Blankinship, be involved with men who kidnap and mistreat women?''

''Morgan had nothing to do with the kidnapping,'' Blankinship said. ''In fact, he didn't know about it until he hit Denver a week ago.''

Vent looked at the others, then asked quietly, ''What about the rest of the combine? They in Denver too?''

''They're there making war talk,'' Blankinship said, then asked, ''Mind if I get up?''

''Get up, but keep your hands away from that gun,'' The Preacher told him.

Blankinship stood, lifted his drink and drained it off. ''Those boys can muster a thousand hard cases if they take it in their heads to do so.'' He looked at Vent and added, ''Not many folks are in sympathy with them, even though you boys did one hell of a lot of damage to their pocketbooks.''

''They'll all be dead before they can muster another ten

men," Arbuckle promised as The Preacher returned his .45 to its holster and, picking up his drink, walked to a table, sat down and stared at Blankinship.

Blankinship tried on a grin. Nobody grinned back. "It might not be that easy to get where you can do that there killin'," he said.

"Where they staying?" Vent asked. "Mr. Blankinship, this here country may be big, but you and me, we both know it ain't that easy for a man to disappear. You lie to us and someday, somewhere, one of us will come up on you and then you're dead meat. You comprende?"

"I ain't no damn fool," Blankinship said. "They're staying in a fancy coach car just south of the round-house on a siding. They got an army guarding the place. If you figure on a showdown there, you better round up a lot bigger bunch than you got now."

"Who's heading up the guards?" The Preacher asked.

Blankinship, still smarting from the old gunfighter's sudden face slapping, refused to look at him, but looked at Vent instead and said, "Whispering Jack Sparks and Butch Bancroft."

The Preacher looked at Vent, then turned and asked Arbuckle, "You know those fellers?"

"I know 'em." The hunchback nodded. "Whispering Jack's from up Montana way. Killed several fellers in a water war up there. They say he's damn fast."

"I heard of this gent, Bancroft," Borden said from his position by the back door. "He worked in El Paso for the Manning brothers. A real hard case."

Glancing at Jenkins, Vent asked mildly, "You want a part of this or are you willing to run your saloon and forget you saw us?"

"I don't butt into another man's fight," Jenkins said.

"When that gambler pulled down on this other gent, I was fixing to get astraddle of him because this here's my place and I don't cotton to fellers coming in here and waving pistols around."

Having delivered himself of this long speech, Jenkins went back to polishing glasses and Borden holstered his shotgun. Blankinship looked at Vent and asked quietly, "You figuring on killing me?"

"What for?" Vent asked.

"Damned if I know, but the thought did kinda creep into my head sorta sideways," Blankinship answered.

"You just ride out, Mr. Blankinship, and if you ride the right direction you ain't got any problems," The Preacher said. "You ride the wrong direction and I'll take that old Sharps off my saddle and plant a blue whistler right between yore shoulders. Comprende?"

"Well, now, that's as plain as all hell," Blankinship said, and walked toward the front door, his back ramrod straight and his arms swinging wide and free from his body.

Watching him go, the hunchback grinned maliciously and observed, "Nervy feller, ain't he?"

Replenishing their grub, the small band of gunfighters rode on west the next morning. As they mounted their horses near the spring, Jenkins came out and, standing near Vent's horse, said, "Mr. Leatherhand, I want you to know you and your friends are welcome here anytime."

Vent nodded. "Why Mr. Jenkins, that's right neighborly of you. I'll remember that the next time I'm out this way," and tipping his hat forward, he led the gunfighters west.

It was hard, rough country and the men rode cautiously, their eyes constantly moving from one piece of cover to

the next as they remained alertly aware of the danger of an
Indian attack. Jenkins had said riders coming through re-
ported seeing small bands of the desert wanderers moving
near the trail. They would appear out of the distant haze,
trot along unconcernedly parallel to the trail, then suddenly
vanish in a swale and not be seen again.

The Preacher continually ranged out to the left of the
group, while Borden, sitting sloppily aslant on the back of
his mule as the stolid animal, seemingly able to travel
forever in his snuffling trot, held down the right flank.
Vent led out in front and twice held up his hand, dismounted and had his look at unshod hoof tracks that
crossed the trail. This was Comanche country and Vent
had no wish to tangle with these grim fighters of the
plains. They were rated as some of the finest horse cavalry
in the world and there was still talk of the Comanche
raids that ranged from Oklahoma to down into Mexico.
The Comanche seemed to have no friends among the other
prairie tribes. They raided indiscriminately and were deeply
feared by their tribal neighbors.

Vent respected them as fighters, as did his companions.
If he could avoid a fight with even the smallest band, he
would.

Two days later found them camping at Cheyenne Wells,
where they replenished their water supply, slept around the
clock, then rode out, heading northwest toward Denver.

The first night out from the Wells, they camped outside
of the tiny settlement of Kit Carson, named after the fame
scout and mountain man, and made Arroyo Springs the
following night. Two more days of hard riding put them
on the banks of the Big Sandy River, where the men
camped in a cottonwood grove and took turns bathing in
the cool waters while three men stayed on guard, taking up

positions in the rocks scattered along the bank of the river and to the north of the grove.

Vent took the opportunity to shave, and as he stood before a scrap of mirror balanced in a fork in a tree and scraped away at several days' accumulation of wiry whiskers, he had a good close look at his face and decided this fight was turning him wolf. I look like a man on the hunt, he thought as he looked into his eyes and saw there the coldness too many dead men had generated. He had seen the same look in Sharp's eyes and The Preacher had it as well. Augustino showed nothing and Borden's eyes were the eyes of a dead man. Arbuckle's half-crazed look was his mark and Vent was certain it had to do with more than his profession. Glancing over at the hunchback, where he lay sprawled on his blanket carefully reassembling his pistol one-handed after cleaning it, he wondered what it would be like to go through life with Arbuckle's handicap. I sure as hell wouldn't have chosen to be a pistol fighter, he thought, and walked to the river and squatted and rinsed the soap from his face.

Using an old shirt to wipe the water and sweat from his face and neck, he walked back up the bank and knelt near the fire, lifted a tin cup and carefully filled it from the simmering pot Arbuckle had left buried in the coals.

As Vent stood up and half turned, the first shot slammed through the grove and Vent felt the sudden sear of pain like a hot nail pass through his left arm. The impact spun him half around and even as he caught himself he was drawing the .44 and firing at a running shadow near the riverbank west of their camp. Then a thundering roll of shots turned the grove into a raging battlefield as gun-wielding riders poured onto the riverbank from half a dozen directions. Wondering where the hell The Preacher, Borden and Augustino had gotten to, and fearing they had been cut down in the first assault, Vent shouted at Sharp to cover the north side of the camp and turned and shot a man out of the saddle as he put his horse up the cutbank from the river in a driving run.

At the first shot, Arbuckle was galvanized into action, whipping out his .45 and firing three times so rapidly, the sounds blended into a death symphony that left three men crumpled in the rocks. Whirling, the hunchback shot another rider from his horse, then a rifleman cut down on him from the trees and Vent saw him jerked around and slammed backward into the bole of a tree. Grinning crazily, he hung there and shot the gun empty, then conjured up a second gun from beneath his flapping serape, and Vent wondered, now where the hell did he get that thing, and was hit again in the right leg, falling down the embankment and into the water.

Struggling to a sitting position, he shoved shells into his smoking .44 and slammed shut the loading gate in time to unhorse a tall rider on a bay who burst over the bank firing wildly down at him. Something snapped in Vent then and somehow he managed to climb back up the bank and rise to his feet just as four riders broke into the camp and jerked their horses up.

"You're dead, Leatherhand!" one of them shouted gleefully, and died instead, as Vent shot him in the face, the heavy slug driving him back and over the rump of his horse. Arbuckle, still in the fight, killed another and Vent triggered twice, sending twin streaks of fire into the bodies of the two remaining gunmen, dropping one directly into the fire. The coffeepot upended and smoke poured from the wet wood and then Sharp whirled into the clearing, leading Vent's Appaloosa, and shouted, "Vent, Borden's dead and The Preacher's on the run. Let's hit it!"

Running to Arbuckle, Vent grasped the gunman under the arms, then cursed wildly when his left arm wouldn't cooperate. Arbuckle looked up at Vent and said distinctly, "Hell of a fight we got goin here, ain't it?" and blood poured from his mouth and he coughed once and was suddenly a dead weight leaning against Vent.

Lowering the hunchback's body, he hobbled to the Appy and swung awkwardly aboard just as two horsemen rode down the bank west of the camp and came through the water at a driving run, their horses' hooves sending sheets of water high in the air. Sharp, his reins held firmly in his teeth, lifted his two guns and fired them simultaneously. The horses rushed on past, their empty saddles mute testimony to the gambler's deadly aim.

As they mounted, Vent looked north and saw Angel Augustino backing toward them, his guns up and blazing as half a dozen riders crowded him. He shot three out of the saddle, then Vent saw his body suddenly jerk backward and at the same instant a hole appeared in the cloth of his jacket at the center of his back and Vent knew he was a dead man walking.

Laughing wildly, the Mexican continued firing as he was struck by several more bullets and then his guns were empty and clicking as Augustino kept cocking them and pulling the trigger. When he finally fell, he twisted around and looked straight at Vent, the eternal smile still on his lips. Then he dropped and Vent whirled the Appaloosa and followed Sharp in a tearing run across the Big Sandy and into the brush on the opposite bank, followed by the screaming whine of bullets as the attackers tried in vain to pick them off before they made the comparative safety of the horse-high mesquite and stunted cottonwood that crowded down almost to the water.

Sharp never let up, leading them at a hard run due west, as the attackers broke from cover and lined out behind them. Vent was grateful for the rest they had been able to give their horses, figuring the attackers, whoever they were, must have ridden a long way that day and were probably mounted on tired horses. He was right. In less than an hour, all but five of the pursuers had dropped out of the race and it was then Sharp, grinning like a gargoyle through the black powder smeared over his face, suddenly swerved his horse into a narrow swale and followed it directly back toward the pursuers. When they suddenly wheeled up out of the cut and pulled in their animals, they were less than fifty feet from the riders and caught them flatfooted.

Panicked, the five horsemen jerked their mounts in and tried to break for the cover of the swale. They never made it. Vent hammered three of them from their saddles and Sharp dumped the remaining two. Riding to where the men lay sprawled in the prairie grass, Sharp stopped near one man who still showed signs of life and as the man looked up at him, asked, "Who sent you?"

"Go to hell," the man said huskily.

"Yore choice," Sharp said, and shot him through the left eye.

They covered another five miles, then Sharp pulled his horse in and walked to Vent and said, "That leg's gonna need treatment, but the arm doesn't seem too bad. Can you move it?"

Nodding, Vent demonstrated and when the pain hit, he ground his teeth to keep from crying out.

Looking at him, Sharp wondered how long it would be before the Missourian's wounds became infected.

Vent, reading his mind, said, "In my saddlebags. They's some whiskey and an old white shirt that'll make bandages."

Sharp helped him dismount and lowered him to the ground, then dug out the whiskey and the shirt, which he tore into strips. He carefully examined both wounds, noting that the bullet had passed completely through the arm but that the wound in the leg still held the slug. Vent watched as the gambler removed the cap from the whiskey bottle and poured a generous amount of the fluid into the leg wound; he cried out in spite of himself. The arm hurt just as much, but he was in better control by then and merely grunted as the sweat burst from his forehead and trickled down his face into the hairs on his chest.

The wounds bandaged, Sharp helped Vent remount and they moved on more slowly, no longer worrying about pursuit.

"What happened back there?" Vent asked.

Sharp, keeping an eye on the prairie around them, said, "Those fellers just seemed to pop right out of the damn ground. Whoever was leading them knew military tactics because he overran us so fast Borden was hit twice before he got off a shot."

Vent recalled hearing the muffled roar of the big man's shotgun during the height of the fight.

"Sounded like he emptied some saddles," he said.

"I didn't count 'em, but some men are riding clouds this day, that I can tell you. Slab Borden did not die easy."

"I never believed he would," Vent said.

Sharp looked at Vent and then said quietly, "Those boys were some of the best, Vent, and they went down.

How long's it gonna be before we wind up riding the same trail?''

Pulling in the Appy, Vent began a cigarette, dropping part of it when he found he couldn't use his left hand very well, and then allowed Sharp to do it for him. With the cigarette in his mouth and drawing, Vent asked quietly, ''You want out of this, Owney?''

The gambler glanced at him, then looked away. ''No, but I know odds. I make my living on them and sometimes I stay alive by keeping track of them. The odds here are just a bit steep for allowing a clean bet.''

''I reckon.'' Vent grinned and, gigging his horse, said, ''What the hell, no gambler is worth his cards unless he's willing to take a long chance once in a while. Hell, Owney, you don't count your chips till the gambling's done.''

They rode on into the night and the next morning found them far to the west of the Big Sandy. Their canteens, filled as was their habit as soon as they had hit the river, were now almost empty and Vent knew they must find water soon. He was beginning to fever up and probably showed it because he had caught Sharp looking at him carefully several times.

They had found Rush Creek and Horse Creek dry, but the towering heights of Pike's Peak, seen clearly in the distance, was a goad to keep on riding.

It was dark as they rode into the front yard of the combination store and saloon at Yoder. The place had been a stopover for wagon trains during the great migrations of settlers who braved Indians, dust storms and outlaws to come west. Now, since the railroads had spanned the vast reaches of that prairie country, it was little more than a resting place for riders on their way to Colorado

Springs and men from some of the cattle ranches in the area.

Stopping in the dark just beyond the splash of lantern light bathing the yard from the open door of the saloon, the two gunmen had their look. A single horse stood at the hitch rail, its head down in half sleep as it waited for its rider, and in a corral north of the main building, Vent counted three horses as they crowded the fence to sniff out these newcomers. The light from a side window reflected off their eyes and Vent, satisfied the place was safe, rode boldly up to the hitch rail and stepped down, almost falling when his leg buckled under him, forcing him to make a grab for the saddle horn. Sharp quickly moved to his side and helped him up the steps and through the door. As soon as they entered the half-dark interior, the gambler left Vent against the wall near the door and stepping to the left, said quietly, "Hello, Preacher. You look like hell."

The Preacher lifted his head and glanced at them, then straightened up and said, "Come on in gents, the water's fine."

"Didn't see your horse out there," Vent said.

"Had to borrow one," the old gambler grunted. "Seems as how my stud got himself lost in the shuffle."

A man came from a back room and when he saw Vent and Sharp, he stopped short and took a careful inventory of them, then said, "Hello, Owney, what the hell you been doing? Eating with the hogs?"

Sharp walked over to the bar and looked at himself in the backbar mirror and chuckled. "You got some water here a man could maybe use to clean up a little?"

Looking at Vent, the saloon keeper observed, "Looks to me like your friend there has a greater need."

Vent, using a chair as a cane, hobbled across the room

and leaned against the bar, careful not to touch his injured left arm. "I could use a drink," he said, and watched as the saloon keeper filled a water glass and slid it in front of him.

"This here's Milo Slade," Sharp said. "Me and him, we been down the trail together."

Slade nodded, then looked at The Preacher and said, "Now this here's like old home week. The Preacher, Owney Sharp and Mr. Leatherhand."

Vent drained off the whiskey and asked, "You got a bed around here," and when Slade answered, Vent did not hear him, but only saw his lips move. Then the floor came up and hit him and blackness claimed him.

Chapter Seven

The railroad car, an ornate coach whose sealed windows were framed with mahogany and whose heavy wooden sides sported the family crest of Deak Hammer—a man whose hard exterior and harder heart belied the sentimentality expressed in the coat of arms—sat on a siding in the Denver railroad yards in solitary splendor. The only thing that distinguished it from others of its type was the heavily armed men who leaned, squatted and lounged about, eyes alert and hands close to guns.

Inside the car five men sat around a green felt table. A pile of poker chips was scattered across the felt. Each man held a set of five cards in his hand and each one's face was narrowed to a fine peak of concentration.

Seemingly unaware of their plush surroundings, the five gamblers made their bets one by one.

Jake Sunderman, short, fat and solemn of mien, sat with a cigar in his mouth, his bulging body filling his chair, and let his fat, ring-bedecked hand drop to his pile of chips, remove ten from the stack and toss them into the middle of the table. "Bet's a thousand," he grunted.

Deak Hammer shrugged his narrow shoulders, brushed a hand through his white hair and fastened a pair of penetrating eyes on Sunderman. His long black coat hung behind him. Around his waist he wore a heavy pistol in a holster suspended from a bullet-loaded shell belt. "Call," he said, and tossed in a handful of chips.

Amos Dewberry shifted his 210 pounds irritably and wondered vaguely why chairs weren't made for big men. Lifting a face that was ugly enough to scare babies—and had often done so in the past—he snuffled in an attempt to head off the nasal drippings from a chronic condition that was irritating to him and usually disgusting to those who met him for the first time. Belching loudly, he snarled, "Bets your thousand and ups it two thousand iron men."

Stiles Burlingame-Leach cocked a cold blue eye at Johnny Tombstone Morgan sitting to his left and asked lazily, "I say, Johnny, you think this blighter's got a hand?"

Morgan looked at the redheaded Englishman and shrugged. The gesture set the stovepipe hat he wore to jiggling slightly; Morgan raised a powerful arm and tipped the headgear back, looked down his nose at his own cards and observed, "If he's got them, they's one way to find out. Call his damn bet."

Leach grinned. Dressed in English tweed, he was the epitome of the refined gentleman, but the others at that table knew the real Leach. They weren't fooled by his offhand manner. He was a shrewd and tough gambler. He called both bets and raised them five thousand more.

Morgan squinted his eyes at his cards, then grunted in disgust and tossed them in. As they snicked across the green felt of the table, the door opened and Tonto McCord entered. He was dirty and unshaven and his left arm was strapped to his stomach and heavily bandaged. His eyes held a bleakness that drew the attention of the five gamblers, who carefully placed their cards on the table and stared.

Walking to the table, McCord heaved three gun belts on top of the pile of chips. One holster held a worn .45. The second rig was a two-gun affair covered with silver and fancy stitching and held two .45s with bone handles decorated with bull's heads. The third rig carried a heavy, sawed-off shotgun.

Reaching out a long finger, Morgan touched a smear of red on the fancy stitching of the two-gun rig and then looked inquiringly at McCord. "Arbuckle, Borden, Augustino," he said deliberately, his gravely voice a grating sound in the close car. "All dead. They died hard. Took eleven good boys with them."

Leach raised an eyebrow. "Leatherhand?" he asked.

"Got away, but we put lead in him."

"The others?" Sunderman asked, but he already knew the answer.

"The Preacher and the gambler got away clean. We sent five boys after them. They ain't come back."

Sunderman, knowing McCord because the gunman had worked for him for almost ten years, asked, "You don't think they'll quit?"

"No sir. They won't quit."

Morgan, more intuitive than the others, looked hard at McCord and wanted to know, "And you?"

"I'm riding out," McCord said, and there was an air of finality to the words. To the five wealthy men, it seemed he was abandoning them to Leatherhand and his gunmen. McCord was their expert. He knew how men like Leatherhand would react to a given situation. They needed him.

"I'll double your salary," Sunderman said.

"Thanks, Mr. Sunderman. Appreciated, but I'm tired of this damn fool game. Good men are dead out there and they'll be more to join them. I ain't worried about myself. I just don't want to be a part of this thing anymore."

Morgan tamped the tobacco into a corncob pipe, clamped his strong teeth around the stem, fired it up, looked at McCord and asked, "Why now? You've been in it from the beginning and God knows, you've never been a man to step sideways of anything . . . why now?"

McCord drew in a deep breath and said quietly, "Mr. Morgan, long after this thing's over and done with, long after Leatherhand and his friends are under the ground, men will talk about this and you five'll be the bad ones. You'll be the ones who'll be looked upon with scorn, with hate. I don't want any part of this. I didn't want it in the beginning, but I earned my pay. Now I quit," and he turned and walked to the door and opened it and started to step onto the rear platform.

The roar of the big six-gun in the close confines of the railroad car was deafening. The .45 slug slammed into McCord's back, drove him out and against the railing on the platform and somersaulted him over it into the dust between the tracks. Several of the guards came running, only to stop and stare at the man lying with eyes open and hand feebly pawing at his chest in a vain attempt to stem the flow of blood from a gaping wound.

"You . . . you bastards . . ." he groaned, and died.

Deak Hammer, smoking gun in his hand, appeared at the back door, looked down at the dead man and said, "Get him outa here," then reentered the car and sat down. "I hate a damn quitter," he growled. "Whose bet is it?"

*   *   *

As the bullet-punctured body of Tonto McCord was being borne away, Vent was fighting the demons of infection in the back room of Milo Slade's saloon, while The Preacher sat near the bed and kept wet towels on his forehead. Sharp had ridden out early to try and fetch a doctor from Colorado Springs. In the saloon, Slade set up drinks for two cowboys in off the range and watched as they gulped them down and nodded for refills.

Half an hour later, the riders left and another man came in and leaned on the bar. He wore a dirty Stetson hat and ragged buckskins worn outside the tops of a pair of neat high-heeled cowboy boots that had seen their share of hard usage. A Mexican serape hung over the man's left shoulder, its ends dangling down to partially conceal the walnut butt of a heavy .44 worn on the left hip and canted over until the grabbing end was almost even with the man's belt buckle. It was holstered in a well-oiled rig attached to a heavy shell belt. A huge bowie hung from his right hip, its blade couched in a beaded sheath of the kind common among the Ute tribe.

Looking at his customer, Slade recognized tough times when he saw them. Here was a man with a lot of hard bark on him, who had been to see the elephant and had spun the wheel of life enough revolutions to know what to expect around the next bend.

"Whiskey," the man said, pushing his dusty hat to the back of his head and fastening a pair of flat blue expressionless eyes on Slade.

"Whiskey it is," Slade agreed, and set up a bottle and glass. He watched as the man poured with his left hand, and thought, gunfighter.

Then The Preacher came from the back room and went and stood beside the stranger; he nodded at Slade and ordered another glass. Slade brought it and watched as the old gunfighter lifted the bottle and poured himself a drink, raised it, said, "Here's to a tight cinch and a handful of aces," and knocked it back.

The stranger drank and then asked, "Vent?"

Nodding his head toward the back room, The Preacher said, "Caught a little lead. Leg and left arm. Running a fever, but he'll live."

"The others?"

"Owney went for a doctor. Coup, Borden and the Mex are riding a cloud somewhere."

"Damn," the stranger said, and there was real feeling in the word.

Glancing at Slade, The Preacher nodded his chin toward the stranger, said, "This here's Charlie Brady. Vent's brother-in-law," and then he turned on his bootheels and led the way to the back room where Vent lay on a narrow cot, his face bathed in sweat.

Brady leaned over him and said softly, "Vent? You hear me?"

Vent opened his eyes, tried on a grin and found it hurt and said huskily, "Trouble with getting all shot to hell. It hurts."

"The other side of the coin," Brady acknowledged.

The sound of horses interrupted them and The Preacher quickly stepped through a back door and was gone. Brady took a position by the inner door, gun in hand. Vent moved his arm from beneath the sheet that covered his sweaty body and bared his .44.

They waited.

Five minutes crawled by and then The Preacher came in from the bar, followed by Sharp and a small man wearing a rumpled gray suit and carrying a black bag.

"This here's Doc Sevege," Sharp said as the little man bent over Vent and peered beneath the bandages on his arm and leg. Noticing the gun, the doctor pursed his lips reprovingly and said, "You won't need that thing, young feller. I've been paid already."

"You need anything, Doc?" Sharp asked.

"Yes, some hot water," Sevege answered absently as he began cutting away the blood-soaked bandages covering Vent's wounds and muttering to himself.

Sharp left and The Preacher and Brady followed suit after watching the doctor for a moment. In the saloon they found Sharp washing the trail dust from his throat with a tall glass of Slade's lukewarm beer and joined him.

Sharp glanced up when Brady came in and asked, "What'd you do with your wife?"

"She's still at the ranch, but the whole damn Ute nation's camped in our lower meadow. They ain't nobody gonna tote her away with Swift Wind's people guarding her, not if they value their hair."

"Decided to cut a piece of this cake, did ya?" The Preacher asked.

"Hell, it's my cake as well as it is you fellers', besides it looks like you've lost half yore army," Brady replied.

"These old boys we're up against got a lot of hard bark on 'em," Sharp observed.

"Well then, I reckon we'll just have to peel some of it off, won't we?" Brady grinned.

The day after the doctor left for Colorado Springs, Vent's fever broke and within three days he was sitting at a table in the saloon letting Sharp teach him how to cheat.

Holding the deck in his hand while The Preacher looked on and Brady sat on the front porch taking his ease, a weather eye out for suspicious riders, Sharp said, "Feller gets good enough with these pasteboards and he can run up five hands on the bottom." As Vent watched he shuffled swiftly, cut several times and dealt out five pat hands, with the highest a royal flush.

Looking at The Preacher, Vent said, "Remind me never to play cards with this gent, especially if I got the mortgage to the ranch in the kitty."

Sharp grinned, flicked a thumb into the middle of the stack of cards and expertly hopped the cut so that the original half that had been on the bottom was now on top. He then proceeded to deal five hands from the top of the deck and each hand was a flush. While they watched he second-carded the deck by swiftly moving the top card back and sliding the one directly beneath it out and dealing it.

Slade came over and served them each a beer. Watching Sharp for a while, he finally turned away, remarking, "Mr. Sharp, you sure come by yore name naturally," and The Preacher grinned frostily.

Looking at him, Vent said, "Preacher, I reckon I'll be ready to move in another two or three days and I got me a little plan."

Sharp shuffled the cards, set them on edge and swiftly fanned them back and forth, then spread them flat-out, faceup, and the cards were in sequence, one through ten and jack, queen, king and the ace lying four deep and in line as to their value. Looking down at this display, Vent whistled. "First time I ever saw a card player do that," he said.

"Took me seven years to perfect it," Sharp replied. "What's yore plan?"

Hobbling to the door, Vent stuck his head out, said,

"Charlie, come in here for a minute," and went back to his chair.

Charlie came in and sat where he could watch the door, then Slade, not a part of this, rose, nodded at Vent and said, "I'll just go outside and sit a spell. See if I can catch some of that west wind." He pushed out the door.

Watching him go, Vent thought, now there goes a damn good man, then turned back and said quietly, "We're gonna become engineers again. I noticed a spur track up there at Dead End. Ran along the main street slam up against the cliff. If that track's clear, we're gonna take our big-time gamblers for a trip to Dead End, only I don't reckon they're gonna cotton to it much."

"There's a lot of guards around that box car," Sharp said.

"I got that figured. We're gonna steal us a train. Then we're gonna get some heavy-gage iron sheets—noticed some once in the railroad yard when I rode through there—and we'll turn that engine into an iron-clad."

Sharp grinned and The Preacher slowly nodded his head as he saw the possibilities in the plan. "We roll her right down the track and buckle her up to that fancy coach car them boy's is playing poker in and just naturally tow it right to hell outa the yards," he observed.

"That's it exactly," Vent agreed.

Brady thought about it for a while, then wanted to know, "How do we stop them fellers from just jumping off the coach?"

"I thought about that and it had me stumped for a while," Vent said, "but then I figured we'd put one man in the engine to actually hook her up. Me, I could take up a position on a building south of the coach just beyond the guards and cover the door with a rifle on that end."

The Preacher nodded. "Every time one of them jiggers sticks his head out, you wang away and bounce a round off the coach, and if one of them gun waddies tries to board her, you send him to hell."

"You've got it figured. We do the same at the other end," Vent told him. "Charlie, you can handle the rifle on that side from the engine itself. We'll just leave a firing slit between the plates and put you there with a box of shells and a Winchester."

"Who handles the train?" Sharp asked.

"How about you, Preacher?" Vent asked, looking at the old gunfighter.

The Preacher nodded. "Sounds like a real fandango," he said and, sitting down opposite Sharp, picked up the cards and casually ran through every trick Sharp had shown them.

"Well, I'll be damned," Vent exclaimed.

"What's my job?" Sharp asked, ignoring The Preacher.

"You open the switches so we got a free run north," Vent said.

Looking at the Missourian, The Preacher said, "You know, Mr. Torrey, what you're planning here is damn near an impossibility? You propose to ride a train right smack dab through an army of armed guards, hook onto a coach and pull her all the way through the Denver switch yards and clean up north to the Medicine Bows. Now I call that high ambition."

Turning cold eyes on the Preacher, Vent said softly, "You're right, Preacher, but I'm going to do her. And when we get to Dead End, I've got a little reception all planned for Mr. Leach and his pards."

After staring at him for a long moment, The Preacher

finally looked away and merely said, "I've ridden this far, I'll ride the last mile."

"You know the rail line north?" Brady asked.

"I know it runs to Loveland and then a spur track goes up into the mines," Vent said.

"That's a hellish piece of railroading back in there," Brady warned.

"Then we'll just have to take her as she lays," Vent said as Slade appeared at the door and said mildly, "Rider comin'."

Vent, Sharp and The Preacher picked up their drinks and the cards and walked through the back door just as a rider jogged into the dusty front yard and went directly to the water trough and watered his horse. Listening by a window, Vent looked at the Preacher and said, "He come aways by the sound of that horse drinking."

Brady, left sitting at the table, rose and strolled over to the bar, leaned against it and casually turned his glass from side to side on the plank, leaving wet rings behind as he waited.

Then the door swung back and a lanky young man wearing heavy bull-hide chaps and worn, runover boots, adorned with a pair of OK spurs, came in fanning the dust from his clothes with a broad-brimmed Texas hat.

"Appreciate it if you'd do that outside," Slade said mildly.

The rider looked up, grinned, said, "Sorry," and went back out.

When he came in again, he had his hat on the back of his head. Walking to the bar, he said, "Set me up a whistle-cutter, pard," and watched critically as Slade filled a glass to the brim. After picking it up, the rider tilted it to his mouth without losing a drop and downed it, then set the glass back on the bar and ordered, "Hit her again."

"That'll be a dollar," Slade said, and waited with the bottle tipped halfway over the glass.

The puncher reached into a chap pocket, came up with a handful of coins and dumped them on the bar. Nodding at Brady, he said, "Give this here feller a drink while you're at it." Then he turned and asked politely, "I'd be pleased if you'd join me. Will you?"

Brady nodded. "Honored, friend," and Slade poured and the two men drank. Then Brady said, "My treat," and paid for two more drinks. Satisfied, Slade left the bottle and went down the plank and began washing glasses, seemingly ignoring the two men.

"Come far, son?" Brady asked.

"All the way from Denver," the man replied.

"Now there's a town that's booming," Sharp grunted, and offered the cowboy his tobacco.

Bending his head over his hands, he rolled a cigarette, placed it in his mouth and accepted a light from Brady, then said, "My name's Will Catlet. . . ."

Brady stuck out a hand and said, "Mine's Rep Hardy," and they shook hands and returned to their drinks.

"Things is a bit rough up there in Denver," Catlet said, and it was obvious he had some news he was eager to share.

Brady cocked an inquiring eyebrow and said, "Oh?" and waited.

"Yep, Deak Hammer—you know him, don'tcha?— plugged Tonto McCord dead center down at the railroad yards four days ago."

Vent, standing near the door in the back room, looked at Sharp and raised an eyebrow. Sharp shook his head.

The cowboy said, "Shot old Tonto right in the back, he did."

"They arrest Hammer?" Brady asked.

"Hell no. Who would arrest him? Not while he's sittin' in that fancy coach of his with a couple of dozen fellers carrying enough guns around there to start the second Civil War, they won't."

"Why would Hammer plug McCord? I heard he worked for them boys. . . ."

The cowboy shook his head. "Beats the hell outen me. It seems since those fellers tangled with that Leatherhand gent and his gunnies they been on the losing side."

"Hell, I heard Mr. Leatherhand lost half his boys in a big fight on the Sandy few days back," Brady said, and poured Catlet another drink.

"He sure as hell did, but they ain't whipped that feller yet. You can bet yere saddle on that. . . ."

"Well, here's mud in yore eye," Brady said, and downed his drink while Vent, who had been counting the drinks, began to wonder if his brother-in-law had a hollow leg.

Catlet called down the plank to Slade, asking for food, and the saloon owner wordlessly picked up a dish and went to the stove, where he filled it with stew made from rich antelope meat and vegetables grown in his own garden behind the combination saloon and mercantile. Stacking half a dozen slices of bread on a separate plate, he carried the food down and placed it on the bar in front of Catlet. "That'll be a dime," he said, and picked up the coin from the pile on the bar and went away.

Sharp watched him eat, not interrupting until he was finished and had sopped up the last of the gravy with the last slice of bread, then said mildly, "You, my friend, were low on hay."

"Been so long since I et, my stomach figured some varmint had slit my throat," Catlet remarked, then called, "Mr. Bartender, that there's the best damn stew I ever got on the outside of. You reckon you could run that horse around the corral again."

Mollified out of his usual solemnity by the brags on his stew, Slade came over, refilled the cowpuncher's plate, glanced at Brady, asked, "You want some of this, Mr. Rep Hardy?" and grinned frostily.

"Looks good, Mr. Slade. Fill her up."

When Slade brought the food he joined Catlet and the two men mopped up their plates wordlessly, then the rider nodded at Slade, pushed a coin out and said, "Buy Mr. Hardy here a drink. Me, I gotta head on east. Me and Paw, we got us a spread over near Wild Horse. Injuns been kickin' up some. Don't like to leave Paw alone too long." He tramped to the door, then turned, and grinning, said, "Paw sent me to Denver special. Said them bawdy-houses there was something. He was right." Laughing, he went out and a few minutes later they heard his horse's hooves drum from the yard, heading east.

Vent came from the back room, followed by Sharp and The Preacher. Looking at Brady, he said, "What you make of that, Mr. Rep Hardy?"

"Damned if I know," Brady admitted, "but it looks like McCord got crossways of them fellers some way or other."

"He was holding cards in a damn rough game," Vent said bleakly.

Three days later, Vent led his men from Yoder and that night they slept in a hotel in Colorado Springs. They rode out again early the following morning for the hard trip north to Denver. Two days put them on the outskirts of the Rocky Mountain city, where they camped at the same springs they had used the last time they were there.

Vent's leg was bothering him so they stayed at the spring two days, giving him a chance to further recuperate and also rest the horses.

It was nine at night when they finally rode into Denver and worked their way through the town to the edge of the railroad yards. Tying their horses in a small copse of trees behind an old hotel serving yardmen and railroad workers, they made their quick inspection of the yards, found the trail they would use and a pile of sheet iron two tracks over that Vent said would make a damn good shield.

"We're gonna need it all the way north," he observed, and Sharp replied caustically, "If we make it out of the yards, that is."

"Pessimistic feller, ain't he?" The Preacher observed.

"It's just that now that I've lifted the old man's mortgage, I'd like to live long enough to inherit the place when he's gone," Sharp said.

"Your inheritance'll be the same as mine," Vent said, and he did not elaborate and didn't need to. His three companions knew what he meant. No man rides by the gun long and lives, they knew, and Brady, grateful for Rhonda, the ranch and his choice of a settled life, knew he was riding tonight with three dead men, knew their time was limited. He looked at The Preacher and suddenly realized the old gambler and gunfighter had given it the lie and Vent, glancing at him, somehow sensed where his brother-in-law's thoughts were taking him, said, "Don't count the tombstones before they're set," and led the way back toward the horses.

Sharp, taking his rifle from the scabbard, left them and walked out the track north from the yard, checking each switch carefully so there would be no mistakes when the action started. He would ride his horse from switch to switch, staying a couple of miles ahead of the train until they were clear of pursuers. He had no doubt they would be followed, then he would board the train. He did not like having to abandon the horses and said so to Vent.

"Hell, that's no problem," Vent replied. "We'll just stick a box car on the back end of that there engine and load up Sharp and The Preacher's horses, and when we get clear of the combine's gunnies, why you and me, we'll load our horses and away we'll go."

The Preacher nodded. "I like that better. At least we got us a way to make a run for it if this here thing comes apart at the saddle seams."

Vent mounted and looked down at them. "Well, let's get that train iron-clad. I want to be able to hook onto the coach by midnight."

Worrying the sheets of iron into place was a tough dirty job and required more time than Vent had allowed, but he knew that without some protection, The Preacher would be dead at the throttle before they cleared the yard.

As they placed the last sheet across the back, a man in an engineer's coveralls and cap came staggering along the track. Spotting them, he walked over and asked, "What the hell you fellers doing?"

"Why haven't you heard?" Vent asked, stepping down and facing the man.

"Heard what?" the railroad man asked, and Vent could smell the liquor on his breath.

"Heard about the territorial governor. He's fixing to

head east and they's a big Injun scare. He wants this engine armored. He ain't a man to take chances."

"Need any help?" the railroader asked generously.

"Why, yes, as a matter of fact you can help us. We need a good solid car to hook onto the front of the engine for the guard's horses. Got any ideas?"

"Foller me, gents," the man said, and led a wobbling path down the track, then stopped and pointed proudly to a high-topped box car sitting on a siding. Vent went to it and had his look, then returned and asked, "What's that tower on top for?"

"Oh, that there's where the guards sit when we ship gold and silver."

Vent grinned and slapped the man on the back and Sharp gave him a cigar and lit it for him.

"We sure thank you, friend, and the governor won't forget this," The Preacher promised.

Nodding jerkily, the man started off, then turned and called, "My name's Olaf. Can you remember that? Olaf . . ."

"We'll remember," Vent assured him, and turning to The Preacher, said, "Get her fired up. We'll hook up to this rig and load you and Charlie's horses right now."

It required half an hour to get the engine ready and another twenty minutes to hook up to the box car and load the horses. Then Vent nodded at The Preacher and said to Brady, "Keep yore head down, old son. I'd never be able to explain to Rhonda if you go and get yourself plugged."

He rode east until he was clear of the yards, stepping his horse along at a slow walk until he had reached the southernmost end of the track-congested area. Pulling the Appaloosa in, he sat and had his careful look, then rode west until he reached a two-story building that housed two engines apparently being worked on by repairmen. Tying the Appy to a pipe near the structure, he walked around it and found a stairway and, carrying his Winchester, climbed it to the flat-topped roof. Moving north, he reached a low parapet and knelt behind it. From this position he had a perfect view of the yard and the luxurious coach squatting in silent splendor by itself on a spur track.

As Vent watched he made out several men sitting on a low platform to the west of the car. Each man was armed with a rifle, and he saw others walking around the coach carrying rifles. A lantern dangled from the rear of the coach and several of the newfangled electric lights cast a bright glow on the area around the platform.

Vent had seen several of these strange and wondrous new lights invented by a man named Edison and brought to Denver earlier that year.

Denver, known as the Queen City of the Plains, also boasted telephones, which Vent discovered were almost impossible to hear anyone on, and electric cars, which were constantly shorting out every time it rained.

But now he was grateful for the added light the bulbs afforded. He saw The Preacher's engine come rolling out of the darkness like a juggernaut, its bulging stack puffing raw, black smoke and sparks flying from the tracks as it scratched for wheel purchase. On it came and when it was a hundred feet from the combine's coach, one of the guards, suddenly alarmed, shouted and ran toward the engine.

Vent let him get halfway there, then slammed a rifle slug into the ground just in front of him. The man shouted and veered away to dive behind a pile of railroad ties.

The train covered another fifty feet before the guards

opened up in earnest, apparently realizing at last what was about to happen.

Clamping his jaw, Vent began firing to hit; his first shot dumped a running man off the platform and into the dirt near the tracks. A lance of fire streaked from the engine and a second man suddenly clutched his stomach and ran sloppily east, his rifle forgotten in the dust behind him.

As Vent pounded out three more rapid shots, a tall gunman collapsed, his hat suddenly spinning away to disappear in the dark.

Then the train slammed into the coach, automatically coupled itself, and The Preacher threw on the brakes and skidded the engine to a stop, reversing it as rapidly as he could. This was the danger point. Vent knew they would be in trouble if the engine balked too long in changing directions.

Streaks of rifle fire shot from behind the platform and from piles of ties as the guards opened up with everything they had. The bullets slapped into the armored sides of the engine, kicking loose sparks from the metal. Inside the engine Brady was answering them, and Vent, watching from his vantage point, saw that the tall ex-marshal seldom missed. Looking far down the yard, Vent saw the shadow of a running horse as it seemingly vanished near a roundhouse, then appeared again further north, its rider briefly highlighted as he galloped past a light pole.

Then the engine was picking up speed backward and Vent watched a man make his try to mount the coach from the rear, let him get onto the platform, then shot him loose and watched coldly as he dropped over the side, bounced on the steel track and was left lying limply between the rails.

As Vent fired at a second man who was making the same attempt, the front door of the coach opened only to draw a hail of bullets from the cab of the engine, where both Brady and The Preacher were firing now.

When the train rolled clear of the lights and Vent knew no one was going to catch it on foot, he quickly crossed the roof and took the steps two at a time. As he reached the Appaloosa, a man materialized from around the corner of the building, a rifle hard against one lean hip, and said tightly, "This is the end of the line, mister." Vent recognized Whispering Jack Sparks and drew like chain lightning loose from hell, fired and watched the look of utter disbelief wash across the man's face as the .44 slug tore into his chest and exited out the back of his vest, which billowed in the wind of its passing.

Sparks screamed then, and suddenly seemed to shrink as he fell, landing flat on his back in a puff of dust.

Vent quickly punched out the spent round, reloaded and swung aboard the Appy; he put him to a run north, swinging wide of the battleground in order to avoid the combine's gunmen.

As he leaped the big horse over a pile of ties, a figure suddenly rose up before him, gun in hand, and fired. Vent felt the hot breath of death as the slug whipped past his cheek to bury itself solidly in the side of the roundhouse.

Whipping the horse in a quick slide to the right, Vent shot the man in the body, heard his agonized grunt, then was away into the night.

He caught the train just as it cleared the edge of town and followed it north at a hard gallop, siding with Sharp, who shouted over the rattle of the engine's wheels against the steel of the track, "We got us a free run all the way to Loveland if we don't meet another train."

Vent, startled because he hadn't thought of that possibility, shouted back, "Reckon one of us better move on ahead and take the high ground, at least for a few miles?"

Sharp nodded and put his horse to a high run and was soon half a mile ahead of the train and gaining as he rode at a sharp angle toward the east, but stayed within easy distance of the track. Vent held his place, watching the doors to the coach, and then, when he estimated they had come a good ten miles from Denver, rode alongside the engine and motioned for The Preacher to pull in.

As the engine slid to a stop, the back coach door opened a crack and Vent, grinning, put a bullet two inches from someone's nose and watched as the door slammed shut again.

Sharp came riding in then and Vent, looking at Sharp's horse, knew the animal had done all it was capable of doing that day and said so. Sharp rode back, lowered the loading ramp on the box car and led the trembling animal inside; he watched as it drank from the tub of water they had filled at the yard.

Stepping down, Vent walked to the coach door; noting it could be dogged shut from the outside, he quickly threw the latch in place and fastened it, then walked along the coach to the back door and locked it as well.

Back at the engine, he looked up at The Preacher and grinned. "Looks like we done caught us some mighty big fish."

"Sorta looks that way," the old gunfighter agreed.

Vent went to the door and called, "You boys in there hear me?"

"We hear you," came the sullen answer.

"You'd just as well make yourself comfortable 'cause you boys are in for a long ride," Vent called.

"Where we going?" a voice challenged.

"All the way to hell," Vent called back.

There was no answer.

Vent led the Appy to the ramp and loaded it, then helped Sharp close the door and climbed aboard the engine, peering over the iron plates to check on its occupants. Brady sat with his back against the side of the cab, a shovel lying on the floor where he had dropped it. He was stripped to the waist and sweat ran down his arms and along his sides.

"Remind me never to take a job as a fireman," he said ruefully, carefully peeling away the hide from a blister on the palm of his hand.

"We got enough coal?" Vent asked.

Looking around, The Preacher, whose face was streaked with a combination of gunpowder and soot from the engine, said, "Hell, I ain't got the slightest notion, Mr. Torrey, sir. Me, I never been an engineer before."

"If we run out, we'll just stop somewhere and take on a new load," Vent replied, and added, "Let's ball the jack, boys, it's a long way to Dead End." He walked back to the horse car, stepped up on its rear platform and went inside. A steep flight of stairs led to the second floor and Vent crawled up there and found Sharp looking north along the right-of-way.

"Hell's angels, a man can see for thirty miles ahead from this here perch," Sharp grunted, and Vent, settling beside him, agreed. Far in the distance the track stretched along the front range as straight as the seam in a dude's trousers. It was clear, and as the train began picking up speed, Vent turned and looked back; he saw the thin line of riders stretched back along the track a mile behind them and, pointing them out to Sharp, observed, "Shore are persistent, ain't they?"

"Hell, we got their paychecks locked up in that coach and the only way they get paid is to spring 'em," Sharp said.

Vent pushed up the back window and shouted down at Brady. When he caught his attention, he pointed south and watched his brother-in-law look out the side of the engine, then nod and go back to shoveling.

"One of us'll have to spell Charlie pretty soon," Vent said.

Sharp made a face, looked at his already soiled black suit, said, "What the hell," and turned back to watch the track ahead.

"How far you reckon it is to Loveland?" Vent asked, watching the riders and noting they were slowly gaining.

"About fifty, maybe sixty miles." Sharp had his look at their pursuers and said, "Those old ponies ain't going to make it. They just haven't got enough bottom for this. Hell, no horse has."

He was wrong. The riders did catch up. Vent watched their leader, a gunman he recognized as Butch Bancroft, as the man angled out away from the track and swung wide, followed by six of his men; they rode toward the north, seemingly ignoring the train.

Lifting his rifle, Vent took careful aim and fired; he watched a rider second in line throw up his arms and drop from the saddle, striking the ground like a bundle of rags and bouncing from view behind a pile of boulders. His second shot unhorsed another rider and then Sharp cut down on Bancroft, deliberately shooting his horse from beneath him.

The gunman kicked his feet loose from the stirrups and,

placing his right palm on the swell of the saddle, let the falling horse's momentum hurl him clear. He hit hard, rolled into deep grass and came up running.

Vent fired just as Brady opened up from the engine and Bancroft stopped, turned around and, standing spraddle-legged, drew both guns and started firing them in a thundering roll of shots that were so closely spaced they seemed like one, then he toppled sideways and Vent knew he had loosed his last bullet.

Sharp unloaded another horseman and Vent dropped two more and they had had enough. He watched as they pulled in their exhausted mounts and sat in a group to the west of the track, staring after the engine.

"They'll hunt up a telegraph somewhere," Vent guessed. Sharp nodded agreement.

They stopped at Platteville. While Vent sat on top of the box car with his Winchester, The Preacher hunted up four men and paid them ten dollars apiece to load the coal tender. While the men were sweating in the ninety-degree heat, a man wearing a star came along the train platform, stopped and, tucking a toothpick in the corner of his mouth, looked up at Vent, then squinted toward the bullet-marked engine with its hastily built armored cab. "Looks like you fellers been in a little war," he said.

"Something like that," Vent replied.

Brady crawled down from the cab and asked the lawman, "Any place around here we can get some food put up?"

"Restaurant just down the street," the marshal said laconically, continuing to watch Vent and his rifle.

Sharp stepped around the rear of the box car and went to the water hose hanging from the siding tank; he loosened it, pushed it through the door and followed it in, saying over his shoulder, "Mind turning that thing on for me, Marshal?"

The marshal nodded and did as Sharp asked, then when Sharp called, "That's enough," shut it off again and moved back down the platform.

The Preacher stepped down from the cab and lit a cigar, then walked over and watched the men shovel coal for a moment, while the marshal watched him.

Taking a last long look at Vent, the marshal turned and started along the platform. Vent said, "Appreciate it if you'd kinda hang around, Marshal. Outlaws might jump us. Could be we would have need of your help."

The marshal stopped and turned carefully, his thumbs tucked under his arms. Vent looked at the two guns the man wore and decided he probably knew how to use them but didn't like the odds.

"Why sure, young feller," he said. "Never know when outlaws may appear on the scene."

The Preacher returned to the engine and waited patiently until the coal tender was full, then handed the men a ten-dollar gold piece each just as Brady returned carrying a boxful of canned food and sandwiches.

"You get some coffee?" Sharp asked.

"Yep, a whole dang potful. Had to pay for pot and all, but damned if it ain't worth it." Brady loaded the food onto the horse-car platform and boarded the engine.

As The Preacher began getting up steam, the marshal walked down until he was directly beneath Vent. He looked up and said, "They telegraphed Loveland. They'll be waiting for you, Mr. Torrey."

"And who might you be?" Vent asked.

"Me, I'm just the town marshal," the lawman said. "Name's Joe Mason."

"From Dodge City?" Vent asked.

"I marshaled there," Mason said.

Vent had heard of him and knew him for an honest lawman. "Thanks, Mr. Mason. It's appreciated."

"Don't like fellers who carry off women and I like men who shoot other men in the back even less," Mason observed dryly. "Good luck," and he turned and left the platform.

Rolling north again, Vent and Sharp ate, then passed the food up to the engine and settled down for the run to Loveland.

Chapter Eight

The Preacher stopped the train a half mile from Loveland
and Vent and Sharp unloaded their horses and rode forward,
entering the mean collection of shacks that made up this
small town hanging on the edge of the front range. Walking their horses down the darkened main street, they passed
several crude stores, a marshal's office, an assay office,
laundry, saddle shop and café. There were no lights and
Vent wondered whether they were riding into a trap.

"No lights," he said.

"Nobody on the streets either," Sharp grunted, and
dropped a hand and lifted off his gun tiedown. Vent
followed suit and they catwalked their horses until they
reached the far end of the town where an ugly livery sat
hunched against the world, fronting a rocky bank. Swinging over, Vent stepped off the Appaloosa, handed the reins
to Sharp and slid silently into the dark confines of the
barnlike structure.

The odor of burned hooves, hay and horse manure

assailed his nostrils as he looked around. Near the back of the building, he saw a thin line of light coming from under the edge of a door and moved toward it, drawing his gun as he went.

Looking back, he could just make out Sharp's tall figure sitting on his horse and could hear the soft metallic sounds coming from the horses' bits as they worried them between their teeth.

When he reached the door, he reholstered his gun and, snakelike, opened it and quickly slipped inside. A powerfully built man with a huge walrus mustache spotted with burn marks, the mark of his trade, sat up in bed and stared at Vent. He had been reading and had apparently fallen asleep. The book was on the blanket and the light had flared up, leaving a long smear of smoke dust on the globe.

"What the hell. . . ?" the man grunted, then reached a huge arm and adjusted the wick. Eyes narrowed, he stared at the lean apparition standing just inside his door and asked again, "What the hell?"

"Howdy, friend," Vent greeted him laconically. "Just rode into your town. Couldn't find a soul around. You folks been hit by the plague?"

Swinging his legs out of bed, the blacksmith pulled on a dirty pair of Levi's and went to a potbellied stove, lightly touched a coffeepot sitting on top of it, grunted with satisfaction, reached to a cupboard above the stove and unearthed two cups. Filling them from the still-warm coffeepot, he offered one to Vent and sat back on the bed with the other. Lifting it, he said, "Here's to gold dust, good women and better whiskey," and gulped half the cup.

Fumbling around under the bed, the blacksmith found a

half-empty bottle and poured a generous amount of its contents into his coffee, held it up to Vent. When he received the gunfighter's nod, he nodded back.

The whiskey had a bite to it, but it helped wake Vent up, helped push him toward even more alertness than he had come into this room with. Now he said, "I asked you if you had a plague here."

"Nope, nothin' like that," the blacksmith answered, gulping his coffee-whiskey mixture with relish and smacking his lips.

"Then where the hell is everybody? It's only nine o'clock."

"Gone to bed, mister. This here town's a quiet town . . . not like them rip-roaring mining camps down south. We got a church and a real honest-to-God sky pilot here. Hell, man, we built us a school last year."

"How many people in this place?" Vent asked.

Scratching his head the blacksmith said, "Well, let's see now . . . last count they was 412 . . . no, now that was before them Arnold boys got into a shoot-out with the Mayberrys and got theirselves kilt. So now it's 410. . . ."

"Any strangers hanging around today?" Vent asked, watching the man's face narrowly.

"Ummm . . . Come to think on it, saw a dozen or so waddies down by the railroad depot. Tough-looking bunch, they was . . . Had a big feller wearing two hog legs and carrying a Winchester rifle-gun in charge. Figured they was some outfit fixing to ship cattle."

"They still around?"

The blacksmith shook his head. "Damned if I know. Me, I got right busy 'bout that time. Old Ernie Dedrick, he came in with a busted-up harness . . . his team ran away agin; I told him he was a damn fool to buy them half-broke

Injun ponies, and then the marshal, he come leadin' that gray of his'n in here and the durn thing had a cracked hoof; these fellers never seem to keep care of their horses' hooves, and after that—''

Vent held up his hand, said, "Thanks, friend. Sorry I woke you," and turned to leave.

"Mister, you best be damn careful out there," the blacksmith suddenly said, and his voice was low and edged with a tightness that carried his fear like a signboard around his neck for all to read.

Vent stopped with his hand on the doorknob, looked back at him and asked quietly, "Why?"

"Those fellers, they said they was waiting for a train to come in. Said some outlaws stole it. Said they was fixin' to have a necktie party, and the big feller, he asked Johnny Hernandez, down at the depot, he's the telegrapher, iffin they was a hangin' tree around close."

Vent grinned and observed, "For a feller who was so all-fired busy you seem to have picked up a lot of information about that bunch."

Draining off the remainder of his coffee royal, the blacksmith said, "Two of them fellers came in to have shoes tacked on their horses. Looked like they'd come a far piece."

"Didn't say just how far, did they?"

Looking at the floor, the blacksmith said softly, "Keep me shy of this mister. I ain't no pistol fighter. I'm just a blacksmith. Me, I don't know who's got the right of it here, but I do know I didn't much cotton to that bunch . . . they said they come down from Cheyenne. . . ."

Nodding, Vent said, "You're out of it and much obliged. Name's Torrey and I don't forget a man who helps me. I owe you."

"I figured who you was, Mr. Torrey. They ain't a man in Colorado who don't know that hand of yourn. Me, I also heard you was a straight one."

"Thanks, mister . . ."

"Baudine . . . Cal Baudine . . ."

"Mr. Baudine, it's been a pleasure. Where would I find this feller Hernandez this time of night?"

Baudine looked straight into Vent's eyes for a long moment and, apparently satisfied with what he saw there, said, "He lives west of town just off the spur line in a one-roomer down there. He's just a kid, but he knows his job."

"I'll remember the part about him being a kid," Vent said, and, nodding at the lamp, suggested, "If you're planning on going back to sleep, you probably won't want that there light on. . . ."

Wordlessly, Baudine reached a long arm, cupped the chimney top in his palm and blew it out with one breath of air without getting up. As he did so, Vent closed his eyes for a long second, then opened them and slipped out into the livery. Walking carefully through the dark interior, he came out and stepped aboard the Appaloosa.

"They was here," he told Sharp. "We go find the telegrapher. He knows which way they went."

They found the mean shack where Hernandez lived and, after Vent hammered on the door several times, managed to rouse the young man, who came to the door in a long flannel nightshirt and stood staring out at the two shadowy figures on his doorstep.

"*Quien es?*" he asked.

"Just a couple of fellers passing through," Vent said. "Need to ask you a question or two?"

"What question?" the telegrapher asked, lapsing into English.

Vent leaned a hard shoulder against the doorjamb and said, "They was a bunch of riders at the depot today. Who were they and where did they go?"

"Who wants to know?" the Mexican demanded.

"Name's Torrey . . . Vent Torrey," Vent said, and waited.

"Mr. Torrey, I work for the railroad. Those hombres work also for the railroad. They come from Cheyenne, where they are employed by Mr. Deak Hammer to protect the Colorado Central against outlaws and Indians. First, I must know what your interest is."

"Simple," Vent said. "I have a difference of opinion with Mr. Hammer. That difference of opinion is a matter of family honor. It is a debt that must be settled in blood, for my sister has been harmed. Do you understand?"

"*Sí*, I understand. I too once had such a matter of honor and because of it, I had to leave Mexico and come to this place. I will tell you. These men said they were expecting some outlaws to pass through here. Said they had stolen a train. They did not say how this was accomplished or why. They said Mr. Hammer wanted his train back and the banditos who stole it hung from a tree limb. The leader, a big hombre they called Vence, he had some ropes with nooses in them hanging from his saddle. Said they were all ready for the train thieves."

"And where did this feller Vence get off to?" Vent asked.

The Mexican came out on the porch, pointed west and said, "He led his men along the spur track. Said he planned to await the train up in the canyon. I wondered how he knew the thieves were going west. . . ."

Vent dug out a twenty-dollar gold piece, put it in the Mexican's palm, said, "Thanks. Buy yourself and some lovely lady a dinner and an evening in Denver sometime," and turned and mounted and led Sharp back toward town.

"*Gracias, amigo,*" the Mexican called, and Vent answered, "*Por nada, señor.*"

"So they're waiting for us, are they?" Sharp said.

"They're waiting," Vent answered, and pushed his mount to a hard trot, keeping the gleaming tracks on his left as they passed through the outskirts of town.

When they could just make out the engine in the light from a quarter moon, Vent dismounted, handed the reins to Sharp and catfooted forward, moving out along the roadbed until he was walking along the edge of a ten-foot drop, figuring if someone had moved in on Brady and The Preacher and was waiting, he'd dive off the edge at the first hostile move.

Nothing happened and when he drew even with the engine cab, Brady said out of the darkness, "You'd never make an Injun, Vent," and chuckling, came up over the edge of the bank and joined him. Turning, Vent whistled softly and Sharp came riding up and dismounted.

"Where's The Preacher?" Vent asked.

"He's asleep in the engine," Brady said.

Thinking about it, Vent decided if the gunmen waiting west of Loveland were going to hit them, it wouldn't be on the main line but after they took the spur line for Dead End. As he remembered, the narrow-gauge track followed a series of canyons in a northwesterly direction, crossing the Cache La Poudre River north of the high parklike area located between the Big Thompson River and the Medicine Bow Mountains. He and Sharp had followed the track for several miles on the way to Dead End; Vent recalled it was a harrowing grade that climbed from about five thousand feet at Loveland to almost eight thousand feet near the Cache La Poudre River.

Making his decision, he said, "We move on west until we reach the spur track, then we switch over onto it and go until we're clear of it by about half a mile."

"Then what?" Brady asked.

"Then we wait until daylight." Vent stepped up on the cab platform, looked over the edge of the iron plating, found The Preacher sound asleep in the engineer's seat. "Time to move, Preacher," Vent called, and the old gunfighter was instantly awake, a hand dropping to his pistol butt.

"Reckon I'm getting too old for this game," he growled, and leaned forward and fired the engine into a slow buildup toward power enough to move it along the tracks as Brady crawled over the plates, stripped off his shirt and picked up a shovel and began heaving coal into the open firebox.

"Now, I know what hell's going to be like," he said as he hurled another shovelful into the fiery maw and watched the flames lick at it eagerly.

Sharp led the horses along the right-of-way and quickly loaded them. With Vent's help, he closed the ramp door and fastened it, then the two men moved up to the rear platform, went inside and climbed the steps to the gun tower.

"You want first watch?" Vent asked, and Sharp said out of the darkness, "I'll wake you when we hit the spur track." Vent lay down on the narrow bench that was fitted to one wall and was almost instantly asleep.

When Sharp shook him awake, it seemed as if he had only been asleep for five minutes, but when he held up his pocket watch and squinted at the dial in the pale moonlight, he saw it was almost four in the morning.

"Where are we?" he asked as he looked out the gun tower window.

"We just left the main track," Brady said, and Vent looked at him sharply and thought, I'm slipping, as he realized he hadn't even noticed Sharp was gone.

"Owney spelling you?" he asked.

"Yep, he's down there practicing for the hereafter," Brady said, and Vent saw the quick shine of his teeth as he smiled. Vent was glad this man had married his sister. He was a man to ride the river with and Vent knew he would stand no matter how tough the fighting was. He only hoped he wasn't leading him to his death.

The Preacher stopped the train then and they all got down and stood stretching as Sharp wondered if they could make coffee on the firebox.

"Hell yes," Brady told him, and went and brought the coffeepot. They filled it with water from a small waterfall, which cascaded down the cliff to pour across the roadbed and drop down the off side into a canyon that was so deep Vent couldn't begin to penetrate its shadowy depths.

The coffee made, they sat around drinking it as the first flush of a new day crawled up the canyon walls and revealed a jagged jumble of towering peaks and timbered slopes so steep they would give a mountain goat vertigo.

Staring around him, Sharp said wonderingly, "Now how the hell did they ever build this damn line?"

"With spit and hope," The Preacher observed.

Vent saw him grimace as he sat the cup down and asked, "You hurtin', Preacher?"

The tall old gunman looked up and Vent found it hard to read his expression because of the soot streaking his face, but his eyes showed pain as he said, "Damn mountain air. It's hell on the rheumatiz."

"Your gun hand?" Sharp asked with genuine concern. All of them knew what happened to a man like The Preacher the day he could no longer conjure up a gun with his old skill.

"I can still use her as good as always," The Preacher said. "It just gives me hell once in a while, that's all."

Staring at him, Brady asked, "How the hell old are you, Preacher?"

"I'm seventy-one," he said without hesitation.

"Well I'll be damned," Vent exclaimed.

"We probably will be before this thing's over," Brady grunted, and stood up. It was full light and time to make plans.

After staring at the cliffs that seemed to hang menacingly over the right-of-way, Vent glanced at Sharp and said, "If I was going to lay for someone and I knew he was riding in an armored train, I'd get up above him and fire down into the cab."

"No protection," Sharp said.

"Up on the cliffs?" The Preacher asked, looking toward the bend in the track where the steel rails curved from sight, following the ragged canyon.

Vent, who was still marveling over the efforts it must have taken to get a line laid into this place, said, "Up on the cliffs. They'll be waiting with rifles."

Then a muffled voice interrupted them from the coach as one of their prisoners shouted, "Hey, what the hell you fellers doing out there?"

Vent strolled back, and, leaning against the side of the coach, said, "Keep your voice down, we're trying to figure out how to get you past a bunch of your hired guns.''

"The hell you say?" Vent recognized Deak Hammer's voice.

"That's right," Vent told him and waited.

"I hope they blow you to hell," Hammer snarled.

"If they do, you're dead," Vent promised.

The Preacher had walked back and now he said, "If they get me, I'm going to pull the throttle wide open before I go down and let that old engine roll. It'll never make the first curve, and where we're settin' they ain't no bottom to the canyon."

Silence was their only answer.

Vent left The Preacher to guard the train and led Brady and Sharp up a narrow crack in the rocks. Armed with Winchesters, they slowly worked their way to the top of the cliff and then crept from rock to rock until Vent suddenly stopped and pointed toward a group of men hiding behind a line of broken boulders a hundred feet below them.

"Like ducks on a pond," Brady said.

"Fish in a barrel," Sharp agreed.

"Notice they ain't got a back door?" Vent asked.

He was right. There was no line of retreat for the men down there if attacked from the rear. It was obvious to Vent the braggart named Vence, the gunman who liked to fashion hang ropes, was not the commander McCord had been, and thinking of the husky-voiced gunfighter, Vent had a small regret for what had happened to him. No man in their profession should go out that way; shot in the back by a man whose only interest in life was making money and gambling. Thinking about it, he decided Deak Hammer was another member of the combine who owed a debt that must be paid.

Watching the waiting men below, Vent did not like the idea of just opening up on them even though he knew they were there to do just that to him and his friends.

Glancing at Sharp, he asked, "Any objection to me giving those boys a chance to quit?"

Brady thought about it as Sharp continued to stare down at the forted-up riflemen.

"Hell yes," he said. "They're down there waiting to open up on us. We should return the favor," but then looking at Vent, Sharp added, "It's your show, Vent. If you want to give those boys a break, it's up to you. I'll ride along with you. It was me, I'd kill 'em."

Brady said quietly, "Me, I guess I'm with Vent on this one, Owney. I ain't that callused yet, even though I know you're dead right, I can't do it."

"Just so," Sharp said, and, grinning, added, "That attitude's gonna get both you boys laid away someday."

Vent nestled his rifle against his cheek and then called down to the hidden gunmen, "Morning, boys. You fellers interested in quitting this game while you're ahead?"

As one man, they whirled around and stared up at the three rifle barrels looking down their throats, then a short, squatty rider grunted disgustedly, "Damn!" and the man called Vence slowly began swiveling his rifle.

"Stop that," Vent said mildly, and the barrel froze.

"Hey Vence, where's them hang ropes you got all rigged up for us?" Sharp asked.

"Go to hell," the man said.

Looking at Vent, Sharp asked, "You got any objections to me and this here man-throttler having us a little private set-to?"

"None at all," Vent assured him.

"You heard the man, hombre. Now drag yere butt out from behind that rock and we'll have us a little party right here. Just you and me."

"I ain't gonna fight you," the gunman said sullenly.

Sharp chuckled, "All gurgle and no guts," he observed sarcastically, and watched as Vence slowly stood up and came from behind the rock.

"Looks like I stung the gent's pride," Sharp said in an aside to Brady.

"I'm waiting," Vence said, and Vent knew he was looking at a dead man.

"Put the rifle on the rock unless that's the weapon you've chosen," Sharp ordered.

The gunman turned and carefully placed the rifle behind him, then said something to one of his men who was crouched against a boulder behind him.

"You there," Brady called. "You sit tight. You move and I'll punch your ticket as sure as God made little green apples."

Vence swaggered out in front of his men and assumed a stance, then waited stolidly as Sharp stood up and stepped from the protection of his rock.

Staring at the man, he suddenly said, "Draw," and watched as Vence made his try.

He was woefully slow.

Sharp waited until the man's gun was almost level with his waist, then drew swiftly and shot him through the left breast pocket and watched him drop, his unfired pistol clutched in his dead hand.

Stepping back behind the protection of the rock, Sharp calmly punched out the empty and replaced it with a live round.

Vent called down, "You can bury those ropes with him. Now drop your rifles and gun belts and move away from them." He watched as the gunmen complied. Once they were disarmed, Vent led Sharp and Brady down to where the defanged men stood against a rock wall awaiting their fate.

One of them, a youth Vent guessed couldn't be over eighteen years old, suddenly spoke up, "You fellers figure you're some shuckins, but this here shindig ain't over yet, not by a damn sight."

Sharp walked over and stood looking at him, then said quietly, "Kid, you keep talking like that and damned if I don't give you the same chance I give your pal there," and the gambler nodded toward the body lying in a pool of blood on the rocks.

"You might find you'd have to draw just a little quicker if you try me," the kid said, and Vent, watching the byplay, thought, There goes another one heading for hell, and wondered what farm or small ranch he came off of. Looking for a rep and tired of being nobody, Vent told himself, and wondered why they did it. He had never planned on becoming a gunfighter, and in the strict sense of the word, he wasn't one now, in that he never hired out his gun. He had wound up a man behind a gun solely because of what the Hawks family had done to his brothers on that fateful day in Kansas. And if it hadn't been for Swift Wind's knowledge of a method to strengthen a ruined hand, Vent knew he would not only never have become a gunman, but would have probably been dead by now, a victim of the Hawkses' bullets. He also knew that if it hadn't been for Cross Tree, the ill-fated gambler who had taught him all the ways of the shootist, he probably would still be practicing on the shores of Lost Lake instead of riding a train into Dead End.

Vent walked over and looked at the kid, then asked, "Boy, you know me?"

"I know you, Mr. Leatherhand," the boy answered.

"What do you know about me?" Vent asked, and was conscious of the other gunmen listening.

"I know you got a big rep, but hell, that don't prove nothin'. Lots of fellers got reps. But then it's easy to plug a few damn fools in the back or rub out a saloon swamper and make yourself look tough."

Sharp chuckled and Brady laughed outright. "Smart mouth on this younker," Sharp observed.

Vent decided it was lesson time. Later, he was unable to explain his actions, even to himself.

"Step out this way kid," he ordered, and led the boy away from the others. Pointing at the pile of holstered weapons, he asked, "Which one of them rigs is yours?"

"The ones with the pearl handles," the kid said, and Vent thought, They would be. He went, picked up the heavy shell belt and noted the pistols were set so that the butts pointed outward and thought, Hickok sure influenced a lot of damn fools, and handed the twin .45s to the kid. "Put them on."

He watched quietly as the kid buckled on the guns, then still watching him, carefully backed off twenty feet and without looking at Sharp, said quietly, "If this kid beats me, you boys let him ride out, but keep a rifle on him so he don't try to spring his friends."

Brady swiveled his Winchester, aligned it with the kid's stomach and stood patiently waiting while Sharp kept the others under his gun.

"Whenever you're ready, boy," Vent said, and there were winter winds in his voice.

"Don't call me boy," the kid snarled, and his hand streaked to his gun.

He was faster than most and Vent guessed that if he lived long enough, someday he would be a man to reckon with, but now he was merely bullet bait for any good gunman.

Vent drew so swiftly that no one actually saw the weapon leave the holster. Without the slightest bit of compassion, he shot the boy through his right elbow and planted a second bullet in his left, shattering them both and leaving him writhing in agony on the rocks near the body of the dead Vence.

Walking over and looking down at the kid, Vent lifted the .44 and leveled it on the boy's forehead and heard the gasp of the men in the background as the kid stared up at the gun through a film of agony.

"Shoot, damn you," he grated, but Vent only lowered the gun and walked away.

"You done him a favor," Brady said, and Sharp, looking at the kid there on the ground, observed, "One he'll probably never appreciate."

"Pick him up and ride out," Vent told the gunmen, and, nodding toward the body, said, "Leave that for the buzzards . . . if they can stomach it."

As the gunmen loaded the whimpering kid on his horse, Vent felt a small regret, but then thought, Better crippled arms than an unmarked grave somewhere, and watched as the gunmen rode single-file east along the tabletop mountain.

Gathering up the rifles and handguns, they worked their way back down the cliff and tossed the weapons into the car with the horses.

The Preacher leaned from the cab and asked, "Have to plug somebody?"

Brady, who was standing near the cab, told him, "Mr. Sharp administered a permanent lesson and Mr. Torrey a temporary one. Now that feller who liked hang ropes is on his way to wherever such fellers go and a kid who thought he was Bill Bonney has a pair of broken wings and a brace of six-guns he will probably live long enough to show off to his grandkids."

It was only then that Vent realized he had allowed the boy to keep his guns.

"What was that shootin' all about?" a voice demanded from the coach.

"Just plugged a couple of fellers you boys had on yore payroll," Brady said.

"Yeah, and now they seem to think the risk is too high," Sharp said. "They hauled off and give us their guns and rode off to punch cows. Seemed to think it's safer."

"To hell with you," Hammer shouted.

"Hammer, if you open yore mouth one more time, I'm gonna come in there and pistol-whip you until yore brain's a whole lot more addled than it is now," Sharp threatened.

Silence followed.

After firing up the engine, The Preacher moved it on along the shelf right-of-way. Looking down from his perch in the guard tower, Vent wondered what would happen if they left the track. Reading his mind, Brady, whose turn it was to ride the tower with Vent, said, "A feller would have time to write his last will and testament before he hit the bottom of that canyon."

All day they crawled up the mountain as Vent, Sharp and Brady spelled each other on the shovel.

At one point The Preacher told Vent, "Coal's getting low. We may not get all the way," and Vent cursed and tossed in another shovelful.

They were five miles from Dead End when The Preacher threw on the air, but it wasn't because they had run out of steam. Vent, who was just trading places with Sharp, leaned out of the guard tower and stared ahead and whistled.

"What's up?" Brady asked, peering past Vent's shoulder. He too whistled as he saw the bridge spanning a narrow canyon. "Hell of a piece of work, ain't it?" he asked, and Vent had to agree.

All that was left was the steel track, part of the under-structure of the bridge and the cross ties, which hung from the bottom of the rails by their spikes.

Vent climbed down, and he and The Preacher walked to the edge of the canyon and had their look. Vent said quietly, "Don't think that'll hold us."

The Preacher walked out on the cross ties and Vent, watching, was surprised to see that they were fairly solid.

"If they're this stout all the way over, I'm game to try her," The Preacher said.

"Hell, man, it ain't worth it," Vent told him. "We can do what we came to do right here."

The Preacher shook his head. "I come this far and damn me, I'm gonna put this rig in Dead End or on the bottom of this here canyon," he told Vent, and Vent knew he meant it.

Looking down into the narrow wedge of cliff-crowded canyon, Vent observed, "It's a hell of a drop down there, Preacher."

"Me, I'm a gambler. I'll take this hand and run with it and the devil take the hindmost," The Preacher said as Brady came up and had his look, as did Sharp.

"You really planning on crossing that?" Sharp asked.

"Yep, I sure as hell am," The Preacher replied.

"That's a dead man's hand you're drawing to," Sharp warned.

"I've taken longer chances," The Preacher said.

"I'll cut the cards with you to see who rides this here bronc," Sharp offered.

"Not my way. I started this run and by God, I'm gonna finish her."

Sharp shrugged fatalistically, knowing talk was useless. "Good luck" was all he said as he walked across the canyon, stepping from cross tie to cross tie.

Vent and Brady followed and Vent decided just maybe The Preacher might make it. He and the others stood on the opposite side of the track and watched as The Preacher backed the train off two hundred feet then slowly allowed it to build up steam. There was no thought of removing the five prisoners from the coach.

Vent could see the old gunfighter clearly as he stood in the cab, hand on the throttle, eyes straight ahead and a frosty grin on his face. He loves this, Vent thought, and in that moment realized what made a man like The Preacher tick. He was just an older version of Arbuckle, Borden and Augustino, and yes, of Owney Sharp. And then another realization came to him.

Hell, me, I'm like the rest of these fellers, he told himself, and it was the first time since he had picked up the gun and began hunting Hawks when he was twelve years old that he was able to admit he belonged to the fraternity of pistol fighters. Then his thoughts were interrupted as the engine rolled out on the ruptured bridge and he watched the track sag under its weight and held his breath.

"Jesus!" Sharp muttered, as the engine somehow kept coming on in spite of the fact that the track had sagged at least three inches.

Vent marveled at The Preacher's iron nerve. Watching him as he stood stolidly in the cab, he saw the old man glance down into the awful maw below him once, look up and grin, and then the train rolled up on solid ground and kept going, dragging the coach and the guard car with it. It was only after the engine and its cars were clear that Vent remembered the horses.

Looking at Sharp he said, "We left the damn horses in there."

"So we did," Sharp said, and lit a cigar, blew smoke into the wind and walked back out to the bridge, then suddenly whirled and ran back away from the edge as the men watched the rest of the structure begin a majestic collapse into the canyon. As it fell away with a roar, its timbers broke like rifle shots and then the whole length of the thing was swallowed up in the maw of the canyon, its going serenaded by howls of inquiry from inside the coach, which were ignored.

"You fellers comin' or do we just sit here and stare into that canyon?" The Preacher asked caustically, and Vent, grinning, clambered up into the guard tower, followed by Brady, who observed, "That old man's got some damn hard bark on him."

"That he has," Vent agreed as the train began moving north again.

Vent, Brady, Sharp and The Preacher sat in chairs along the verandah of the hotel and watched the coach. The sun had crept behind a cloud and the canyon was in shadow, the only movement the horses stamping their feet where

Brady had tied them to a corral fence across the small creek.

The Preacher, looking at it, said, "Ya know, I rode herd on this here town for three years and helped put a few headboards up there on the hill, but none of that means doodly-squat now. It's all dead and gone and I can't even remember them fellers' names."

"I know what you're saying," Sharp replied. "I once downed a man in Abilene and didn't realize I had never heard his name until I was twenty miles from town."

Brady glanced at Vent, then asked, "Vent, can you recall the names of them fellers that jumped me in Creede when you took a hand?"

Vent thought about it for a moment, then shook his head. There were others on his backtrail whose faces he couldn't remember, let alone their names. After a while, it seemed, they all blended into one man with a gun facing you on some cowtown street.

Looking at the coach, Sharp asked, "Well, now, Mr. Torrey, you done caught your fish. When you planning to put them in the skillet?"

"I'm thinking on that," Vent replied, staring speculatively at the coach, which now sat by itself in the middle of the town. They had uncoupled the engine after pushing the guard car to the end of the track and leaving it there. Then they hauled the coach back to the center of town. After dropping it off, The Preacher had gotten up a good head of steam and, pulling the throttle open, left the engine.

Thinking about it now, Vent said, "That damned engine sure made a hell of a bang when she dropped off into that canyon, didn't it?"

The Preacher grinned. "That there's one train they ain't gonna get back," he avowed.

Vent rose and walked to the edge of the verandah, where he stood staring at the coach, thinking, If I was Coup Arbuckle, I'd just set her on fire or open the door and shoot those fellers down like the dogs they are, but knew he couldn't do it. Instead, he turned to Sharp and said, "We're gonna play a little game with these boys."

"A game?" The Preacher asked, looking sharply at Vent.

Vent walked down to the coach, drew his gun, tapped on the side of the car, and called, "You in there, listen to what I've got to say because I'm only going to say it once."

"Go to hell," Hammer responded.

"Sunderman, you hear me?" Vent called.

"I hear you, Torrey," Sunderman replied, his voice loud and harsh.

"I'm gonna give you fellers a chance; more of a chance than you gave us," Vent said.

"Don't do us any damn favors," Hammer snarled.

"Hammer, if I hear one more damn word out of you, I'm gonna pull you from that car and hang you from the livery-barn gate," Vent snapped.

"Listen, old boy," Leach called. "Maybe we can make a deal. Suppose we each put up the full amount you fellows would have won had you gone through with the contest and you let us leave. Now that's fair, isn't it?"

"It is if you can figure a way for us to send Arbuckle, Borden and Augustino their shares," Sharp called.

"Can't help them. They're dead," Leach said reasonably.

Vent looked away for a moment, then walked around to the door and said harshly, "Leach, you come out of there and you come alone. And Hammer, you toss out that gun you like to use shooting fellers in the back, and any other guns you got in there."

A minute dragged by and then Leach said hesitantly, "I'll come out if I have your word you won't kill me."

"I ain't gonna plug you," Vent promised, and undogged the door, then stepped clear, drew his gun, called to Sharp, "Owney, if Hammer tries something stupid, kill them all," and waited.

Sharp picked up his rifle, walked to the edge of the verandah and stood waiting, the weapon held against his right hip, bearing on the door.

Leach slowly opened the door and came out. Vent called, "Hammer, toss out the weapons and do it now or I swear to God I'll dog that door and dynamite the car."

Then Morgan came to the door, pushed it boldly open, stepped onto the platform and dropped four guns into the dust. Looking at Vent, he said, "Torrey, I don't know what you got planned, but if you kill us, you'll be outlawed all over the West, you and these friends of yours."

Vent, looking levelly at Morgan, said, "If I decide to kill you, Mr. Morgan, they ain't gonna be anybody but us four who'll know it and you've been around enough men like these to figure they ain't gonna talk."

Vent, watching Morgan's face, saw the acceptance of this crawl into his eyes and with it a lost hope. It was apparent he thought he and the others were going to die. That realization made him reckless as he thrust out a blunt jaw and snapped, "Well, if this here's to be the killin' ground, Mr. Torrey, then get on with it."

Sharp chuckled and The Preacher said softly, "Send out Hammer," and waited until the lean, cadaverous figure of the banker moved out onto the platform and stood defiantly facing them.

"They say you're a pretty fair hand with a gun, Mr. Banker," The Preacher said, and his voice was as smooth as silk. As Vent listened to him, the hair on the back of his head almost stood on end and, looking at the others, he realized the old gunfighter's words were having the same effect on them.

Hammer stared at The Preacher as if mesmerized. He couldn't seem to speak and Vent watched as he swallowed several times in the attempt, then The Preacher stood up and suddenly he wasn't seventy-one years old anymore. His walk had turned into a prowl as he moved off the verandah and across the street. His shoulders were some-how wider and gone was the negligent slouch he so often affected. In its place was a self-assured march to some drummer out of the past.

They all watched the black-clad figure move to the bottom of the steps then reach inside his coat and bring forth a Bible. He opened it and read in a loud voice, " 'For these be the days of vengeance, that all things that are written may be fulfilled,' Luke twenty-two. 'And they shall fall by the edge of the sword, and shall be led away captive into all nations,' Luke twenty-four. 'For what is a man advantaged, if he gain the whole world, and lose himself, or be cast away?' Luke twenty-five." He snapped the Bible closed and bent and picked up Hammer's gun belt and said, "Come, Mr. Hammer, and prepare to meet your Maker . . . or maybe they'll save the cost of transport and send you directly the other way."

During this brief sermon, Hammer had stood as if rooted to the train platform, but now he moved down the steps; when he reached the last one, he stumbled and was forced to clutch at the rail to save himself from falling.

Raising a long, black-clad arm, The Preacher extended his finger, pointed to the middle of the street, said in a sepulchral voice, "Out there, Mr. Hammer," and tossed the gun belt into the dust.

Hammer bent and picked it up and buckled it around his waist as if he were following words engraved in stone, then looked at The Preacher, waited, and suddenly there were tears in his eyes. Instead of the hard old banker, they were staring at a man whose will to win had completely vanished, leaving behind an empty shell.

"Well, I'll be damned," Sharp exclaimed.

"Are you ready?" The Preacher called, turning so that he faced Hammer squarely. He either did not care that he was facing a beaten man or had deliberately programmed the fight to accomplish the destruction of the banker's will.

"Yes," Hammer said huskily, but he did not look at The Preacher nor did he touch his gun.

"You're killing an unarmed man, you know?" Morgan suddenly said.

The Preacher did not look around, but instead casually drew his left-hand gun and, flipping it in line with the banker, fired and watched clinically as Hammer's hat was plucked from his head and sent spiraling away to disappear behind the false front of the assay office.

The second shot blew away one of Hammer's bootheels, almost knocking him off his feet, and the third shot struck the man's gun at the hammer and sent it tumbling end over end along the street.

Watching the gunplay, Vent knew he was seeing one hell of a display of marksmanship and was glad he had never been forced to come up against this old man in his youth.

Sharp, tiring of the scene, said quietly, "He's done for, Preacher."

Nodding, The Preacher punched out his empties and

reloaded the .45, dropped it into his holster, and, walking to the banker, said, "Take off your boots."

"What?" Hammer asked dazedly.

"I said, take off your boots," The Preacher ordered again, and watched as Hammer sat down in the dust, carefully removed his boots and set them side by side and stood up again.

Pointing down canyon, The Preacher snapped, "Walk," and watched as Hammer, still in a daze, turned and trudged off down the street, seemingly impervious to the sharp stones he was stepping on. Staring after the gaunt, white-haired figure, Vent knew he had just watched a man being broken by an expert.

Leach and Morgan looked at the retreating figure and then Morgan said harshly, "Why the hell didn't you just kill him, Preacher?"

"All men are eventually held responsible for their actions, either in this world or the next," The Preacher said solemnly, then walked to the verandah, turned and added, "Your time will come, Mr. Morgan. . . ."

"And so it will be with you too," Morgan replied, and The Preacher nodded, said, "Just so," and went inside the hotel.

Vent watched him go, then turned back and said, "You fellers seem to enjoy playing high-stakes poker, so we're gonna give you a chance to demonstrate just how high you can roll."

Morgan raised an eyebrow, then Dewberry and Sunderman came hesitantly out on the platform and stood listening as Vent said, "You boys are going to play a game of poker for the highest stakes you ever played for."

"What kind of stakes?" Dewberry asked, then, not

having been on the platform during the breaking of Hammer, looked around and wanted to know, "What happened to Hammer? You fellers kill him?"

Vent pointed down canyon where Hammer was just turning the corner of the trail and said, "He decided to walk back."

Then Dewberry saw the banker's boots sitting in the middle of the street and drew in a long shaky breath and said, "Bare-footed, huh?"

Vent nodded.

"Damn!" Dewberry exclaimed. "He'll never make it."

"It was more of a chance than he gave McCord," Sharp said harshly.

Vent, watching Morgan and Dewberry, knew the two understood Sharp's feelings, but it was obvious neither Leach nor Sunderman knew why Sharp felt the way he did.

"Why would you care what happened to McCord?" Leach asked reasonably. "Hell, he tried to kill you men."

Sharp said, "That's just the point, Mr. Leach. McCord was a square fighter. He took his chances and he earned his pay. When he decided the game was no longer worth playing, he tried to cash out and Hammer killed him . . . by shooting him in the back. Think on that. If one of you fellers want out of a poker game, you just quit. You don't have to worry about somebody shooting you over it."

"That still don't make sense," Leach protested. "We play poker. McCord was hired to do a job. He quit in the middle of it."

Sharp sighed. "Mr. Leach, that's just it. You boys' game is poker. McCord's game was fighting. He had as much right to quit his game as you have to quit yours."

Vent said then, "Mr. Morgan, you understand Mr. Sharp's point, don't you?"

Morgan nodded. "He's right, Stiles. McCord should have been allowed to leave without interference. I told you boys at the time, Hammer was going to regret that. Well, if he lives through a fifty-mile walk in his bare feet, he will probably never forget it."

Vent stared hard at Leach, then said, "Mr. Leach, you kidnapped my sister. Out here in the West, that's a hanging offense. Me, I don't much care for hangings, but I'm toying with the idea of stretching your neck because there's usually an exception to every man's rules and God knows you're it."

Leach raised a shaky hand to his face and said, "Mr. Torrey, I'm truly repentant for that unfortunate action. I have nothing against your sister and would not have harmed her even if you had refused to take part in our little game."

"Mr. Dewberry, what about your actions in buying up my father's mortgage and threatening to put him out of his home?" Sharp suddenly demanded, and Vent realized he had completely forgotten the reason for Sharp's involvement in the deadly lottery devised by the combine.

"I wouldn't have done it," Dewberry protested.

"How the hell do we know that?" Sharp asked.

"I reckon you don't and I can't prove it now, but I swear by all that's holy, I'd never have put that old fellow out."

Watching him, Vent was damned sure Dewberry would have done just the opposite and now he said so. "Dewberry, you're a damned liar. You would have tossed old man Sharp out on his ear and you, Mr. Leach, have a lot to answer for in regards to my sister, but I'm going to allow

Mr. Brady here to have you. It was his wife you kidnapped and mistreated.''

Brady walked over and stood looking up at Leach, then said, ''Mr. Leach, I'm told you're quite the hand fighter. Is that correct?''

''I've done a bit of boxing,'' Leach admitted, and Vent saw the sly look creep into the man's eyes and knew he was probably very good at it.

''Step down here and let's try you out,'' Brady said, and his mouth peeled back in a flat grin as he removed his gun belt and tossed it to Sharp.

Leach came down the steps confidently, removing his jacket as he moved out into the street and dropping it in the dust. Then he turned and stood facing Brady with his hands on his hips.

Brady strolled over and faced the Englishman. Leach raised his fists in a defensive posture and, bending his legs at the knees, began a slow sideways shuffling around Brady, who stood with hands down, watching him carefully. He was not fooled by the awkward-appearing stance, Vent knew. Pugilism was a popular sport in the West during that period in time and almost everybody had watched at least one bare-knuckle fight. It was obvious Leach had done his share of boxing.

Suddenly his right fist lashed out and Brady slipped to the left, neatly dodging the blow, then lashed out with a savage roundhouse, only to fan the air as Leach, countering with a hard left, struck him in the mouth, jarring his head back and drawing first blood. The Englishman followed it with a right that connected with Brady's ear, cracking loudly enough so that Vent flinched with the impact. Brady's head rocked, then his left fist came out of nowhere and buried itself in Leach's stomach; the tall, lean mountain man followed it up with a smashing right that slammed into the hinge of Leach's jaw, driving him to his knees.

Vent thought he was finished, but Leach was apparently in a lot better shape than he appeared to be. He came up off the ground and hammered a right and left and another right into Brady's face, knocking him off his feet.

Brady didn't stay down long. Coming up from the ground, he drove his head into the pit of Leach's stomach, smashing him into the side of the coach with enough impact to actually jar the thing. Vent, watching Leach's face, saw his mouth stretch wide in agony, then somewhere he managed to call up a reservoir of strength and scrambled sideways, turning as he did and driving a hard right into Brady's chest just under his heart. The blow carried considerable steam and Vent wondered where the hell the man was getting it from.

Brady staggered back, then hit Leach in the face with a terrible blow, and Vent saw the Englishman's nose flatten and blood gush down the front of his shirt as he growled deep in his throat and came on again, his head between his shoulders, his fists still up and in their proper position.

"What the hell's keeping that feller up?" The Preacher wondered. He had come from the hotel at the beginning of the fight and was now standing just behind Vent.

"He's got him a lot of hard bark," Vent observed as Brady knocked him down again. As he lay on the ground gasping for air, Brady stepped back, dropped his arms and, hanging his head, did his own share of pulling in air. Watching Leach, Vent was astonished to see him sit up and begin fumbling with the top of his right boot. He almost missed the stingy gun the Englishman pulled because the man's hand hid most of it, but the sun's rays caught part of the metal, and as he suddenly lifted it and pointed the deadly derringer at Brady's head, Vent drew as swiftly as he had ever pulled a gun in his life and fired a split second before Leach jerked the trigger. As it was he was almost too late.

The heavy .45 slug tore its deadly path through Leach's chest just below his heart and knocked him sprawling, but not before he managed to fire the hideout gun. Its heavy .44 slug hit Brady in the fleshy part of his left leg, passed on through and struck the front of the marshal's office with a solid crack.

Brady's leg was jerked from beneath him and he fell heavily, then rolled over and clutched the leg. Vent hurried to him as Sharp walked to the dying Englishman, stared down at him and said, "Now that was a stupid thing to do."

"A man must preserve his dignity," Leach said, and died.

Looking up at the remaining members of the combine standing openmouthed on the platform, Sharp asked, "Any more of you boys interested in preserving your dignity?"

They wordlessly shook their heads.

Half an hour later, Brady was resting comfortably in an upstairs room and Vent was again standing, facing the three remaining members of the combine.

"Gentlemen, here's the only key to your opening a way out of this town," he said. "You're going to play a game of poker and each man is going to place his entire holdings in the pot in the form of a written statement, leaving it to the winner of the game. Now, it's up to you fellers how you go about it. You can bet a ranch at a time, a bank at a time or a railroad or whatever, but gamble you will."

Morgan stared at Vent. "You mean you expect us to gamble away all our holdings?"

"That's right," Vent assured him, and Sharp chuckled softly from the hotel verandah. The Preacher stood stolidly watching.

"What the hell's to stop us from giving it all back once the game's over and we're away from here?" Sunderman asked.

"Simple," Vent told him. "If you try that, I'll hunt you down and kill you."

Morgan stared at him and it was apparent he was remembering all that he had heard about Vent and had no doubt the Missourian would keep his promise.

Reading his mind, Vent said softly, "You can bet your life I'll do it, Mr. Morgan."

"I believe you," Morgan said simply, then turned and looked at Sunderman and Dewberry and said, "Gentlemen, shall we play poker?"

The game was played in the hotel lobby, where Sharp and Dewberry set up the table from the coach and provided paper and pen from the same source.

When the three men were seated around the table, Vent said, "Gentlemen, Mr. Sharp will deal. You may proceed. May the best man win."

Dewberry, his tiny eyes appraising his fellow players shrewdly, waited for his cards. Sunderman, his fat body overflowing his chair, chewed his cigar and watched Sharp shuffle the cards. Morgan flexed his powerful fingers, raised a hand and scratched his three-day-old growth of gray whiskers, tilted his stovepipe hat over one eye and said calmly, "I been waiting for a game like this all my life."

Chapter Nine

It was five A.M. and the first flush of dawn cast its glow down the dusty main street of Dead End, highlighting the false fronts of the buildings and reflecting off the broken shards of glass littering the wooden sidewalk in front of Harrington's Haberdashery.

Vent's Appaloosa raised its head from the creek, and, water dripping from its jaws, stared at the hotel with ears pointing forward like semaphores. Then the object of his interest stepped from the building, paused on the front verandah and began rolling a morning cigarette.

Inside, Sharp, his face not yet showing the strain of having dealt cards for nine hours straight, flipped out three more hands and said, "Gentlemen, play the game."

Vent, hearing him, grinned and dragged deep on his smoke, then walked back inside just as The Preacher came from a back room carrying a trayful of beef sandwiches and sat them down on the felt of the keno layout. Morgan was saying, "I'll bet my hotel in Tombstone," and squinted at his cards.

Dewberry called with a restaurant in Denver. Sunderman folded.

The game had seesawed all night long as the three wealthy men placed their fortunes on the turn of the cards, seemingly unaffected when they lost a silver mine or ten thousand head of Montana-raised cattle. At present Morgan led the others in acquisitions, but Sunderman was running him a close second.

The Preacher went back to the kitchen and returned with a large coffeepot and a trayful of cups; sitting them on the keno table, he intoned, "Food's here, gents."

Morgan won the hand and rose as Sharp shuffled. Pushing his stovepipe hat back, he helped himself to two sandwiches and a cup of coffee and returned to the table. Sunderman, watching him bite into the thick, meaty concoction, swallowed, then rose and went to the table and picked up his own sandwich, raised it to his mouth and in half a dozen huge bites devoured it.

Sharp looked up and observed, "Mr. Sunderman, it's not for me to comment on another man's eating habits, but it strikes me that if I ran an eating establishment, I'd insist that you take your meals in a back room by yourself."

Dewberry squinted his pig eyes, then fetched himself a sandwich and coffee and absently pushed it bite by bite into his mouth while peeking at the cards as they slid across the table to stop in a neat row in front of him.

Sunderman, who had refused to answer Sharp, picked up another sandwich. It vanished behind the first. Then he burped, grunted and sat down again.

Vent picked up a sandwich, poured a tin cup full of coffee and strolled out onto the verandah again, where he sat down in a chair and, leaning back against the wall, idly watched the horses as they fed along the creek bank. Then his Appy raised its head and looked south and Vent was instantly alert. Finishing his sandwich, he drank off the coffee, rose and reentered the hotel lobby, his back braced against the slamming impact of a bullet.

As he cleared the doorway he nodded at The Preacher and led the way up the stairs into Brady's room. The mountain man was asleep, but instantly awoke when the two entered the door.

Looking at Vent's face, he asked quietly, "What's up?"

"Horses watching something down canyon and it ain't deer," Vent said, and, walking to the window, carefully moved the rotting curtain away and had his look.

Nothing moved out there, but his hunter's instinct told him they were being stalked. The Preacher felt it too, and picking up Brady's rifle where it rested against the wall, he came over and put it on the bed. Nodding at Vent, he went to one end and, with Vent at the other, helped move it to where it rested just under the sill, giving Brady a sweeping view of most of the town.

There was no glass in the window and the frame had long since fallen away, leaving a solid resting place for Brady's rifle.

Touching him on the shoulder, Vent said, "Watch. If anything moves down there, use your rifle butt to tap on the floor," and received Brady's nod and led The Preacher back downstairs.

As they entered the lobby Sharp looked up, raised an eyebrow inquiringly and dealt a card to Morgan, who promptly bet a sawmill near Creede and was called with a one-eighth interest in a railroad by Dewberry and three hundred head of horses by Sunderman.

"Better get a bite, Owney," Vent counseled, and, nodding, the gambler rose and walked to the keno table, followed by Vent and The Preacher.

"We got company," Vent said softly.

"How many?" Sharp asked, biting into a sandwich. He seemed unconcerned.

"Haven't seen them yet," Vent answered, and Sharp did not question that there was somebody out there. He knew Vent's senses had talked to him, just as they were talking to him now.

"Me, I been feeling antsy for quite a while," he said.

The Preacher prowled to the back door and slipped out. Sharp returned to the table, but this time he slid his chair around until his back was to the wall and picked up the cards.

The three players looked at each other, then Morgan, who was much more perceptive than the others, asked quietly, "You expecting trouble, Mr. Sharp?"

"Something like that," Sharp said, and began dealing the cards.

Morgan turned and stared at Vent, who was standing just to the right of the front door, his leather-bound hand resting on his gun butt, the tie dangling down the side of the holster. "Boys, it looks like some of those fellers we hired are bound and determined to earn their money," he said, and Sunderman and Dewberry looked up, suddenly all ears.

Vent glanced around and said quietly, "If we're hit, gentlemen, I suggest you get behind the bar and stay out of this. If you don't, you'll be the first to go." Then he glanced back down the street and saw a man run from the blacksmith shop to a partially collapsed lawyer's office and dive from sight, his rifle gripped in his right hand.

"They're down there," Vent said just as Brady tapped lightly on the floor above.

"Know who?" Sharp asked as The Preacher slid back into the lobby and answered the question for Vent.

"Same bunch we defanged down on the right-of-way," he said. "Must of rode to Loveland and bought guns."

Sharp shrugged. "That's what happens when you leave loose ends. We should have gunned those varmints."

"Little late for that now," Morgan observed.

"Oh, I wouldn't necessarily say that," Sharp countered.

The Preacher picked up his rifle from the top of the bar and, nodding at Vent, said, "I reckon I'm going hunting," and left by the back door again.

Sharp folded the cards and said, "Gentlemen, we're calling a little moratorium on this here game. Table's closed." He gathered up the pile of signed papers that the three combine members had used to back up their bets and stuffed them into his pocket.

Morgan, watching this maneuver, asked, "What happens if you get plugged, Mr. Sharp?"

"Why, I reckon I'll just up and bleed all over your property deeds," he said, and walked to the front door and had his look.

"Shall we let them come to us?" he asked.

Vent glanced at the cardplayers and said, "Behind the bar, boys. I reckon it suits me better to take the fight to them." He drew his .44 and went through the door on the run, dropped off the verandah and, whirling down street, hammered off two shots and watched a lanky gunnie suddenly topple from an alley and land on his face in the dust. He did not stir.

With Vent's shots the town of Dead End suddenly erupted

into a shooting gallery, with him and his friends the clay pigeons.

"Let her rip!" Sharp yelled as he broke through the front door and, guns fisted, blasted slugs into a storefront, tearing a dying scream from somebody.

Doubling over, Vent ran across the street and dove down an alley, then raced along behind the buildings as Brady opened up from the hotel's second floor. Firing as he ran, he was sure he tagged at least two men before his cover ran out and he was forced to take refuge behind a pile of rotting cross ties near the railroad track.

As half a dozen slugs hammered into the ties Vent saw a man backing from an alley, then the cloth of his jacket suddenly bulged outward and three holes appeared in it as if by magic. The force of the impact hurled him into and over a water trough. The Preacher, a .45 in each hand, appeared briefly in the alley, pushed back his wide-brimmed black hat with a pistol barrel, then whirled and was swallowed up by the darkness of the passage.

Shots came from the assay office and someone with a Sharps rifle was up in the big house on the hill, firing down into the street. With each booming shot Vent heard the eerie wail of the huge slug as it tore the air apart on its way to the center of the town. When the slugs struck something, they made a loud chunking noise. Vent, looking up at the sprawling house once frequented by old Silas Carpenter, the man who founded Dead End, knew he was going to have to eliminate the sniper or sooner or later he would kill them all.

Two more shots sounded and the logs shook as the slugs hit them. Vent cried out in simulated agony and then moaned loudly, finally cutting it off as if he were finished. Then he waited, grinning at his playacting, and, when no more bullets pounded into his refuge, broke cover and ran to the rear of the old Chinese laundry as someone shouted, "Hey," and tossed a hasty bullet after him.

Looking north along the rear of the buildings fronting Main Street, he was in time to see a man run out on one of the bridges spanning Bobcat Creek. Lifting his .44, he shot the runner in the right side and watched him topple off the bridge and into the water, where he slowly floated facedown to the first riffle.

Brady's rifle boomed twice from the hotel; a man ran from another alley and, blood pouring down his shirtfront, pitched into the creek, joining Vent's victim.

Running north now, Vent almost shot The Preacher when the black-garbed old gunman burst from an alley and turned toward him. They met halfway along the main street and Vent, noticing blood on the ex-marshal's shirt just under his rib cage, asked, "You hit, Preacher?"

"Took a piece of hide is all," The Preacher said, but Vent, noting the tight jaw muscles and the white face, knew it was more than that.

"Why don't you fort up in the old jail;" he advised. "It would take a dozen sticks of dynamite to winkle you out of there."

Nodding, The Preacher turned and moved rapidly north, ducking from sight as he entered the back door of the solidly built log jail. There was a shout from inside the structure, then The Preacher's .45s roared twice and a man staggered from the building and ran headlong into a tree on the creek bank. Grasping it, he slowly slid to the ground, dropping his pistol into the creek.

As Vent ran past him he looked up and said, "Oh Jesus, help me . . .." and Vent ran on, ducking behind a line of boulders at the head of the main street. Using them for cover, he worked his way west until he was almost level with the big house. Crouching behind a rock, he stared at the building and then somebody moved in an upper dormer window, followed by the thundering roar of the Sharps. Again the .50 caliber screamed down the slope and Vent heard it smash into the back of the hotel.

As he watched, Sunderman suddenly broke from the back door and ran awkwardly up the slope toward the house, waving a white flag. He was fifty feet from the hotel when the Sharps spoke again. The heavy slug struck the running fat man in the stomach and tore out his back, lifting him off his feet in the process and dumping him end over end back down the slope where he pitched up against a broken fence and did not move.

"Damn fool," Vent grunted, and suddenly broke cover, racing for the back door as the rifleman tried desperately to swivel his weapon and bring it to bear on the running figure. He didn't make it and Vent dove through the back door, raced up the stairs just as the man appeared on the landing, and fired, knocking him backward and off the balcony. He landed in the huge front room with a crash and lay still.

Walking to where the Sharps lay, Vent picked it up and, moving to the window, had his look, grinned, raised it and centered the big bore on a man crouched near the back of one of the half-dozen saloons in the town, then carefully squeezed off a shot. The bullet kicked the man off his feet and into the tall grass near an upended privy, and Vent, looking around, noted a pile of shells on a nearby table and quickly fed another round into the single shot's chamber and took up his vantage point again.

He was in time to see three men rush the jail. All three went down under The Preacher's deadly guns. Looking back at the hotel, he saw two men approach the back door, sent a Sharps round into one man's body and watched with satisfaction as the second man whirled and ran to an alley and vanished from sight.

Vent couldn't see the front of the hotel but knew The Preacher had a good view of it and that Sharp was probably in position to keep tabs on their prisoners.

Then he saw the gambler step from the Overland Stage Company office, guns palmed, and fire first to the right then the left at somebody Vent couldn't see. As the gambler raised his gun for a third shot he was hit and knocked back inside the building. Vent cursed, threw away the Sharps and dove down the stairs. Racing down the slope, he ducked along the back of the west side of the buildings and each time a man appeared, fired, watched him fall and ran on. A shot from an alley laced a spear of agony along his left side, spinning him around and almost knocking him off his feet, then he righted himself, shot and a man screamed high and wild and died in a doorway, his face blown away.

Later he could never recall that final ten minutes of the fight, but he knew he must have shot his gun empty and reloaded at least twice. He left half a dozen dead and wounded men behind him and somehow wound up back at the stage office, where he discovered Sharp sitting on the floor in a pool of his own blood, leaning against the wall, his left-hand gun in the dirt beside him, his right fisted and pointing at the door.

"Where you hit, old hoss?" Vent asked, bending over the gambler.

Sharp, his face tight with pain, said between his teeth, "They keep shooting me in the meaty part of my shoulder. I've been nailed there twice before."

Pulling away the cloth, Vent saw it was a nasty wound but decided the gambler would live and told him so.

"Damn!" was all Sharp said.

"I reckon," Vent said, and went to check on The Preacher. He found him leaning against the wall of the old jail and asked, "How you, Preacher?"

"I'll make her." The old gunman gazed around at the unused jail. "I always wanted to lock a man up in here but never got the chance."

"Fight's over, but we best keep an eye open crossing the street." Vent led the way back to the stage station, where they helped Sharp to his feet and the three of them made their shaky way to the hotel lobby.

No shots greeted them as they moved out into the street, then Brady looked out the window and Vent called, "You see anything, Charlie?"

"Not a damn thing now," Brady replied. "Several fellers ran down canyon and I spotted a horse handler bring their mounts to them. Reckon they lit a shuck."

Inside the hotel they found Morgan sitting at the table staring at the cards scattered over the felt.

Vent glanced around, then asked, "Where's Dewberry, Morgan?"

Lifting his chin toward the bar, he said, "Back there," and Vent went and had his look and found Dewberry lying dead, a huge hole obviously made by the Sharps in his throat. Not only had the slug severed his windpipe, but it had also blown away his spinal cord.

"That last shot," Vent said.

Morgan sighed, then looking at the three bloody apparitions standing before him, observed, "You fellers look like you been in a fight."

Sharp drew his .45, cocked it, leveled it at Morgan and said softly, "I think I'll just make this a round robin."

Morgan looked down the barrel but did not flinch.

"Go ahead, gambler," he said. "I'm quitting the game so I reckon this is as good a time as any to go out."

Sharp stared at him. "Quitting . . . why?"

"Hell, man, I'll never again find a game like this one. It was the ultimate in poker games. Who the hell wants to live after this?"

Sharp holstered his gun with a sour grin and said, "Reckon you're right, Mr. Morgan. I don't figure you'll ever see another game like this one," and he drew the papers from his pocket and handed them to Morgan, who glanced down at the sheets, each with its "To Whom It May Concern" scrawled across the top of the page, and below it a statement of what was being bet and the notation that whoever had the paper in his possession could legally lay claim to the property.

"You giving up several million dollars, Mr. Sharp?" Morgan asked, a puzzled expression on his face.

"You won her fair and square, Mr. Morgan. You're the survivor. Me, I'll win mine the same way," and then he turned and walked away, but stopped at the door to the kitchen and, looking down at his bloody side, asked, "By the way, how the hell did Deak Hammer ever manage to catch a man like McCord off guard long enough to kill him?"

Morgan grinned sourly. "Why that's easy. McCord had a mangled-up hand. It seems that stud of Coup Arbuckle's damned near bit it off."

Chapter Ten

Two months after the gunfight at Dead End, Vent led Sharp, The Preacher and Brady back to Lost Lake. They were met in the front yard by a wildly squealing Rhonda, who flung her arms around Brady's neck and kissed him soundly while peeking over his shoulder at her brother, who sat the Appaloosa and watched approvingly.

Swift Wind rode out of the timber and pulled his magnificent horse to a stop in front of Vent and nodded solemnly. "Leatherhand, you return," he said.

"A little older and a little wiser, my friend," Vent replied as he stepped stiffly from the saddle.

Watching him, the Ute shaman nodded his head sagely and said, "I talked with the gods four moons ago. They told me you were in a great fight far to the north and that you had been injured, as had your companions. There were many coups counted and scalps were taken. It was a great victory."

"Well, Swift Wind, I ain't certain sure it was a great

victory, but we did win.'' Vent grinned as Rhonda came, put her arms around his neck and hugged him and, leaning back, observed, ''You have three more gray hairs, brother.''

Extricating himself, Vent nodded at The Preacher, who was slowly puffing on a cigar, and pointed out, ''Hell, The Preacher there, he's got him a whole head of white hair and it ain't slowed him down none.''

The Preacher grinned frostily and dismounted. Sharp, favoring his side, stepped down too and, taking the horses' reins, led them off to the corral while the others entered the house.

Rhonda quickly fixed an evening meal and the men ate silently, Swift Wind sitting in a place of honor at the head of the table. When the meal was over, coffee cups were filled, then Rhonda asked, ''What happened, Vent Torrey? You must tell me the story.''

Vent filled her in, then described the fight at Dead End and the role her husband played in it, noting, ''When the smoke cleared away, they was a few empty saddles and several gents with holes in them who still lived.''

''You didn't just leave them there, did you?'' Rhonda asked, and Vent, remembering the aftermath of the fight, recalled how Sharp had said harshly, ''Let's put these bastards out of their misery,'' and how he couldn't find it in his heart to shoot wounded men.

Instead they had left Morgan to tend them and rode to Loveland, where help was sent back. Holing up then in an old boardinghouse near the railroad, they were taken care of by the owner, a woman who had nursed her share of gunshot victims back to health.

When they were ready to ride out again, Vent led his small band of gunfighters along to the Loveland marshal's office and found a U.S. deputy marshal there sitting in a chair, his back against the wall, his feet up on the railing facing the street.

Nodding, Vent said, "I'm Vent Torrey. These here fellers are The Preacher, Owney Sharp and my sister's husband, Charlie Brady."

Inclining his head slightly, the marshal said, "Gentlemen, I'm Paden Tolbert, U.S. marshal for this here part of the country."

Tolbert appeared to be still in his teens and Vent, gazing at his boyish face, thought, I must have looked like that when I first came to Colorado. "Marshal, you may have heard we had a little set-to up at Dead End with some fellers," Vent said. "Had to put some of them down. You got any problem with that?"

Sharp lit a cigar and blew smoke past his horse's ears. The Preacher grinned frostily. Brady removed his foot from the stirrup and let his injured leg dangle, easing the strain on it.

Tolbert carefully rolled a cigarette, then plastering it to a lower lip, said, "None, gentlemen. Besides, I couldn't find a jury in the West who would convict you fellers, not after what the combine did to you."

"Just so," Vent said. "We bid you good day," and he turned and started away and Tolbert stood up and said, "Mr. Torrey, I got me a question?"

Reining in the Appy, Vent swiveled in the saddle and looked at the marshal and waited.

"How many men went down in this fracas?" the marshal asked.

Vent thought that over, then said softly, "Too damn many, Marshal Tolbert," and led his friends down street and out of town.

Now, sitting at the big table in the cabin at Lost Lake,

Vent retold the fight story to Rhonda and tired, sought his blankets, leaving The Preacher and Sharp to tend the horses. Soon they carried their bedrolls out under the stars and bedded down for the night.

Two days later, Vent rose early and built up the fire, heated the coffee and, carrying a steaming cup to the front porch, was in time to watch Sharp and The Preacher ride from the corral.

Looking at them quizzically, he asked, "You boys heading somewhere?"

"Down the trail," Sharp answered.

"Over the hill," The Preacher said.

Vent grinned. "See you sometime," and he rose and leaned against a porch support and watched them ride down the meadow and stop at the edge of the timber, turn their horses and sit quietly looking back. Then Sharp raised an arm and waved it nonchalantly and The Preacher doffed his black hat and bowed far over in the saddle, straightened back up, replaced his hat squarely on his head and disappeared into the timber, followed closely by Sharp.

Brady had come to the door behind Vent and now he said, "A couple of good men . . ."

Vent took the trail to the lake, where he found the old log where he once practiced his deadly gun art while Swift Wind looked on. Now the Indian came from around the lake on his Appaloosa and reined in and said, "How, Leatherhand."

Vent, face solemn, answered, "How, Swift Wind," and watched the quick shine appear in the Ute's eyes.

Swift Wind sat and looked at Vent for a long moment, then said softly, "You and I, old friend, will meet another time. Our trails have not yet run their courses, but watch where you tread, for the miles ahead are filled with bad spirits.'' He reined the horse away and loped him around the lake, paused to lift his rifle above his head in a final salute, then was gone.

Vent walked to the meadow above the ranch and stood for a long moment of silence looking down at the grave of Lilly Tree. A small board had been placed at her head and Vent knelt and read the inscription.

''Here Lies Lilly Tree, the Beloved of Vent Torrey. May They One Day Meet in Heaven,'' it said, and Vent guessed Rhonda had carved the epitaph and set the marker.

Early the following morning he said his good-byes and turned the big Appaloosa down through the meadow and onto the Crested Butte road. The wind shook fall leaves from the aspens as he jogged along. Reaching behind the cantelboard, he untied his windbreaker and shrugged into it, carefully lifting the skirt clear of his gun butt and letting his hand rest there for a long moment.

Then with grave deliberation, he allowed the past into his head, watching the parade of ghostly faces pass in review, and accepted the responsibility for their dying.

Shrugging, he smiled, but it did not show in the cold, quiet eyes as he allowed the Appaloosa its head, tucked his chin deep in his collar and flipped a mental coin, watching it land on an imaginary arrow pointing south.

Four days later, he crossed into New Mexico just north of Shiprock as the sun came out from behind a cloud and sent its beams streaking along the trail toward Sante Fe.

He followed the sun.